Thankful Sweets

Connie Shelton

Books by Connie Shelton

The Charlie Parker Mystery Series

Deadly Gamble
Vacations Can Be Murder
Partnerships Can Be Murder
Small Towns Can Be Murder
Memories Can Be Murder
Honeymoons Can Be Murder
Reunions Can Be Murder
Competition Can Be Murder
Balloons Can Be Murder
Obsessions Can Be Murder
Gossip Can Be Murder
Stardom Can Be Murder
Phantoms Can Be Murder
Buried Secrets Can Be Murder
Legends Can Be Murder
Weddings Can Be Murder
Alibis Can Be Murder
Escapes Can Be Murder
Sweethearts Can Be Murder
Money Can Be Murder
Road Trips Can Be Murder
Cruises Can Be Murder
Old Bones Can Be Murder - a Halloween novella
Holidays Can Be Murder - a Christmas novella

The Samantha Sweet Series

Sweet Masterpiece
Sweet's Sweets
Sweet Holidays
Sweet Hearts
Bitter Sweet
Sweets Galore
Sweets Begorra
Sweet Payback
Sweet Somethings
Sweets Forgotten
Spooky Sweet
Sticky Sweet
Sweet Magic
Deadly Sweet Dreams
The Ghost of Christmas Sweet
Tricky Sweet
Haunted Sweets
Secret Sweets
Spellbound Sweets - a Halloween novella
Thanksful Sweets - a Thanksgiving novella
The Woodcarver's Secret - prequel to the series

The Heist Ladies Series

Diamonds Aren't Forever
The Trophy Wife Exchange
Movie Mogul Mama
Homeless in Heaven
Show Me the Money

Children's Books

Daisy and Maisie and the Great Lizard Hunt
Daisy and Maisie and the Lost Kitten

Thankful Sweets

A Samantha Sweet Mystery Novella

Connie Shelton

Secret Staircase Books

Thankful Sweets
Published by Secret Staircase Books, an imprint of
Columbine Publishing Group, LLC
PO Box 416, Angel Fire, NM 87710

This book is a work of fiction. Names, characters, places and incidents are either the product of the author's imagination or are used fictitiously. Any resemblance to actual events or locales or persons, living or dead, is entirely coincidental. Although the author and publisher have made every effort to ensure the accuracy and completeness of information contained in this book we assume no responsibility for errors, inaccuracies, omissions, or any inconsistency herein. Any slights of people, places or organizations are unintentional.

Book layout and design by Secret Staircase Books
Cover images © Makeitdoubleplz, BooksRMe

First trade paperback edition: November, 2024
First e-book edition: November, 2024
* * *

Publisher's Cataloging-in-Publication Data

Shelton, Connie
Thankful Sweets / by Connie Shelton.
p. cm.
ISBN 978-1649141897 (paperback)
ISBN 978-1649141903 (e-book)

1. Samantha Sweet (Fictitious character)--Fiction. 2. Taos, New Mexico—Fiction. 3. Paranormal activity—Fiction. 4. Bakery—Fiction. 5. Women sleuths—Fiction. I. Title

Samantha Sweet Mystery Series.
Shelton, Connie, Samantha Sweet mysteries.

BISAC : FICTION / Mystery & Detective.

813/.54

For you, my readers, with thanks.
I am forever grateful.

Chapter 1

The Sangre de Cristo mountains loomed ahead, a welcome sight to Samantha Sweet as she and Beau left the open grasslands and flat prairie behind. She reached across the console in his pickup truck and took her husband's hand.

"For two kids who grew up in the flatlands, we sure miss the high country when we're gone, don't we?"

"We do. And I'll tell you, two weeks back in my hometown … that was plenty." Beau took it slow through the town of Cimarron, where it was well known that speeders were not tolerated.

"Is it awful of me to say that I'm not unhappy Cecelia didn't take us up on our invitation for Thanksgiving?"

He laughed. "Not a bit. I love my family, but I'm ready for a break. Cece reminds me, in a lot of ways, why I never had a particular hankering to move back to Oklahoma."

"She's had a rough time, and you know I'd do anything for her …"

"But it's fine that she had other family to spend the holidays with. I completely get it."

"It's just that I'm going to be swamped at the bakery. I know Jen's been taking pie orders and Becky and Julio have been doing as much as they can ahead of time, but a lot of it's last-minute. This coming week is going to be crazy."

"And I'm sensing a yearning to stop by there on our way home," he teased.

"If you don't mind …"

"I don't mind a bit. It's been a long drive and maybe we can grab tacos or something to take home for dinner so neither of us needs to cook."

"And this is why I love you so much." She adjusted the visor so the late afternoon sun wasn't quite so bothersome.

Beau steered expertly along the winding canyon road, and roughly ninety minutes later they were approaching Taos Plaza from the east. Rush hour meant there were nearly a dozen cars at the traffic light, everyone eager to get home on this Monday afternoon.

Sweet's Sweets glowed with soft interior lights and the purple awning picked up the dusky tones of sunset. Sam smiled, loving the little business she'd built. Three cars sat out front and she could see Jen at the counter, serving customers with a smile.

Beau pulled around to the alley behind the short row of businesses and stopped behind the bakery's delivery van. Sam barely waited until the truck came to a full stop before she had her door open. He gave a rueful grin and followed her inside.

Julio was washing some baking sheets at the sink. "Hey, boss. How was your trip?" The tattoo on his left arm flexed as he lifted a large sheet and directed the rinse water at it.

"The drive went fine, and we're glad to be home," Sam said. She meandered toward her desk and picked up the stack of order sheets, getting a quick feel for what lay ahead in the coming days.

"I've got a bunch of pie crusts baked, ready for fillings. Tomorrow's delivery day for the big doings."

Sam's mind went blank. Big doings?

Jen pushed through the curtain that divided the kitchen from the sales room, her face glowing. "I thought I heard your voices." She rushed over to give Sam a hug, then one for Beau.

"Remind me," Sam said, "how many pies are we delivering?"

"Oh, for the Harvest Feast?" Jen said. "One dozen ten-inch pumpkin, I think it was."

"Right." Julio set two pans on the rack and dried his hands. "Well, I'm done for the night. See you all tomorrow, bright and early."

He adjusted the bandanna on his head, picked up his leather jacket and went out. A moment later they heard his Harley rev to life.

Sam rubbed her temples and turned to Jen. "I'm really embarrassed to admit this, but what harvest feast? Did I know about this?"

"Oh gosh, you probably never got the details. I am so sorry." Jen seemed distressed. "Nancy Whitson, that lady from the Chamber of Commerce, came in a day or so after you guys left for Oklahoma. She's come up with this idea for a big town-wide Thanksgiving weekend celebration, something to feed those who are food-insecure and to bring out the aspects of bounty, sharing, food, and camaraderie. Sort of the antidote to all the Black Friday hoopla, to put the focus on something other than standing in line outside Walmart to score a deal on a big screen TV."

"I love the idea, but isn't it coming up a bit close to the deadline?"

Jen took Sam's hands and squeezed. "The posters are all over town, but I guess they went up when you weren't here. You'll see them. And there's a lot of hype on the radio and in the *Taos News*. It's turning into a pretty big deal."

Beau had moved toward the sales room, and Sam told him to grab some brownies or cookies if he wanted to take something home for dessert.

"So, we're donating pies for this event. Anything else we can do?" Sam's eyes took in the shelves of inventory, estimating.

"That's all they've asked from us," Jen told her. "In return, the business will get lots of publicity and be listed as an official sponsor. Our name will be up there along with some really well-known chefs. According to Nancy, they've got professionals from all over the state and each is featuring their signature dishes, some will even teach cooking classes and give out samples. Hernando Rodriguez is one of them." Her eyes went a little wider.

"I may not get much TV time, but even I know that name. Isn't he from Albuquerque?"

"Born and raised there, studied in New York, has a James Beard Award and more than one Michelin star to his credit. His restaurants in Santa Fe and Albuquerque have waiting lists for reservations."

"Impressive."

"Yeah, apparently Nancy Whitson has connections."

"I hope local restaurateurs also get some press attention?"

"Me too. It does seem to be a focus, and one of the reasons why it's worth it for us to donate the pies." Jen raised her eyebrows. "I thought Becky ran all this past you in one of your calls?"

"I'm sure she did. I probably spaced it out. Things in Oklahoma got a little intense." Uncovering a massive embezzlement scam, figuring out what happened to several missing persons, and solving a murder—yeah, a little distracting from her real life.

Beau came back into the kitchen with a small paper bag. "Peanut butter for me, a brownie for you. I called ahead to Macho Taco and Rueben is getting an order together for us." His eyes looked tired.

"We gotta go, get this guy home and get some rest for both of us," Sam said. "You'll lock up?"

"Got it all under control. We're glad you're back, Sam."

They stepped out into the chilly dark and Beau started to circle the truck to Sam's side.

Next door, the back door flung open and Riki Davis-Jones, owner of Puppy Chic and Kelly's employer, rushed out and stumbled down the steps to the alley.

Sam looked up, started to wave hello, and noticed Riki was sobbing uncontrollably. "Riki? What's the matter?"

The two of them crossed over to their friend in distress.

"Evan's leaving me!" Her shoulders shook. "It's really official."

Chapter 2

Sam pulled Riki into a hug. So, maybe this was what was behind the young British expat's recent moodiness (according to Sam's daughter who had confided). She looked beyond Riki's shoulder toward Beau. *Sorry*, she mouthed as she pulled a clean tissue from her jacket pocket.

"Can we help?"

Riki shook her head as she wiped her nose. "Not unless you can talk some sense to my hardheaded husband." A deep sigh. "No, that's not exactly it, either. I'm at that stage where I need to vent, and luckily Kelly has agreed to meet me for a drink where I shall get all of this off my chest and be as good as new tomorrow."

"Are you sure that's the best thing?" Beau asked, concerned.

"Probably not. But Kelly has also said she would drive

me home and tuck me in if I require an escort." She gave a weak smile. "I may have a banger of a headache tomorrow but this, as all things in life, will work out somehow."

"Leave your car here and we'll drop you by wherever it is you're meeting Kelly," Beau said, in his no-nonsense lawman voice.

Riki nodded. "Give me five minutes to lock up my shop."

An hour later, Beau was unlocking the front door at home. Sam carried bags of tacos, their dessert, and the couple of tote bags she could sling over her shoulders. They could do the real unpacking in the morning.

While the tacos rewarmed and Beau poured himself a beer, Sam texted her daughter to let Kelly know they were home, although it was probably superfluous. Asking if Riki was going to be okay, she got the reply: Yep, in time.

After dinner, Beau decided to walk out to the barn to check on the horses and touch base with Danny Flores, his hired man who'd been caring for their two dogs for the past two weeks. Sam cut her brownie in half and brewed a cup of chamomile tea. She tossed the taco wrappers in the trash, set the brownie on a napkin, and headed for the living room.

A fire would be nice, but she had the feeling they would both be ready to head upstairs in an hour or so. No point in getting a roaring blaze going this late in the evening. As she walked past the bureau near the coat closet, she spotted a blinking red light. A message on the landline phone? It was such a rarity these days, she seldom even looked at the machine.

She pressed the play button and stood there, expecting a solicitation of some kind, which she would immediately delete. But the voice that came through was somewhat familiar.

"Beau, it's Tim Haskins. Wonder if you could give me a call? On my cell? It's kind of important, so as soon as you can. Thanks." He recited a number. Click.

Huh. Why would the mayor be calling? Sam saved the message and carried her dessert over to the sofa, where she sank into her favorite corner and let out a long sigh.

The front door opened as she was plucking up the last crumbs of the brownie, and the two dogs bounded toward her.

"Ranger! Nellie! Settle down," Beau commanded.

But the black Lab and border collie were beyond excited to be back home with their humans. Sam pushed her tea mug to a safer spot and reached down to bestow hugs and tickle their ears.

"Everything looks good outside," Beau said. "I'm so glad we found Danny when we did. The kid still has a lot of energy like I used to, at his age. Is there any hot chocolate?"

She directed him to the cabinet with the packets of cocoa mix. "Sorry, I don't have the energy to make it fresh right now. Plus, there's no milk until I make a grocery run tomorrow. Oh—you'll want to listen to the answering machine. You have a message from the *mayor*."

"Yeah, you tease me, but he's probably running for reelection and wants a donation," he muttered, heading toward the kitchen.

Sam had thought the same thing, but this wasn't the normal time of year for campaigns. Oh well, Beau would find out soon enough. She snuggled back into her corner, her eyelids drooping. When he emerged from the kitchen, two peanut butter cookies and a mug in hand, she realized how tired she was.

"I'm heading upstairs. If I'm lying prone on the bed and my eyes are closed, you can assume it's better not to talk to me because I won't remember a bit of it." She smiled and gave him a kiss.

It was actually less than ten minutes before she heard his boots on the stairs. She'd changed into her favorite comfy sleepwear and was brushing her teeth when he appeared in the bathroom doorway.

"Well, Haskins isn't looking for donations," he said.

She rinsed and stared at him.

"He wants a new sheriff. And he wants it to be me."

Sam felt her mouth open and shut a couple of times. "What—?"

"It seems Evan Richards has taken another job, out of state, and he's leaving immediately."

"Whoa. Okay, so now we know why Riki was so upset. Well, part of it, I guess. Do you suppose she's going with him?"

"Sam, did you get the main point of this? Haskins wants *me* to be sheriff again. My old job."

"Can he do that? You were elected to the position."

"Right. But the mayor has the authority to appoint an interim sheriff until the next election."

"What did you tell him?"

"That I'd think about it. I mean ..." He ran a hand through his thick, graying hair. "I'm surprised. I would have thought he'd offer the job to one of the deputies. Rico's got a lot of years with the department now, and he's still young. Couple of the other guys, Padilla or Lawson."

"Honey, hold on. What about *your* feelings? Do you

want the job?" She'd seen the way he lit up at times during their recent case in Oklahoma. Being a lawman was in his blood, she'd realized.

"I don't know, darlin'. I'm fifty-five now. How long can I continue to be effective?"

"That's not what I asked, and it's not what the mayor asked. Do you want the job now, for however long that entails?"

"I gotta sleep on it." He turned toward the bedroom, but she knew from his smile that he was completely tempted.

Chapter 3

Despite the news, Sam fell asleep the moment she pulled the comforter up to her shoulders. Her dreams were filled with pie recipes and images of a worktable full of rolled crusts. When she awoke at a little after one a.m., she realized Beau's dreams must be equally active. He was murmuring in his sleep.

She used the bathroom and went back to bed but realized there was no way she would get back to sleep. Maybe five hours of sleep would hold her. She chose her customary black slacks, white t-shirt, and white baker's jacket from the closet and carried them into the bathroom to dress. Her carved wooden box sat on the vanity where she'd unpacked it from the tote she'd brought it home in.

"Okay, buddy, help me out here. This is going to be a busy one." As the wood warmed and turned to its golden color, she felt energy surge through her arms.

Half an hour later she was staring at the worktable from her recent dream—a dozen pie crusts were rolled and trimmed to fit their pans. She'd fired up the large bake oven the moment she walked into Sweet's Sweets, and now she fitted the pie plates onto a tray and inserted them. Soon, the scent of warm dough filled the air as she blended pumpkin, eggs, cream and spices for the filling.

A second batch of dough was soon ready, more crusts formed, and as the pumpkin pies went in for their baking time, she reviewed the orders from her customers. Apple with a lattice crust, apple with crumb topping, cranberry-apple, pecan, and blueberry topped the list. She measured ingredients and filled pie crusts, losing track of time in the process.

By the time Julio arrived at six, the cooling racks were filled with finished pies and another dozen fruit pies were in the oven.

"Somebody didn't sleep last night," Julio joked, as he donned his apron and asked what Sam wanted him to do next.

While he started the bakery's normal morning assortment of muffins and quiches, Sam decided she'd better take a break. She'd forgotten exactly how much her handling of the wooden box sped up her process; the result always raised eyebrows.

She walked out to the quiet sales area and started brewing the first pot of her signature blend coffee. Outside, the sky held the faintest tinge of morning light, and she could tell full daylight was coming soon. Inside, soft night-lamps gave her little shop a warm glow, highlighting the bistro tables and the baked goods in the display cases.

She saw Becky's car at the far side of the parking lot, and she went to unlock the front door for her chief decorator.

"Wow, you're early," Becky said. "I can smell pumpkin pie already."

"Hard time sleeping. It must be jetlag."

"You were one time zone away and you drove home." Becky pulled off her gloves and unbuttoned her coat. "But, I'm not complaining. The next couple days are going to be insane, and I'm happy we can get a jump on it."

"Coffee's ready. I was about to pour myself one."

"Yes, please, me too. I rushed out of the house this morning, not quite fully awake. Left Don to get the boys ready for school." Becky headed toward the kitchen while Sam carried the two mugs.

They settled into the morning routine, with Jen arriving to open up for the customers whose morning habit included a pastry and coffee before work. They had a couple dozen regulars who always helped start get the shop's day off to a positive start.

Becky boxed up the pumpkin pies for the Harvest Feast, setting them aside, then started a new round of baking to fill customer orders. Most would pick up their pies tomorrow, so those would go into the fridge once they were fully cooled. Sam's oven-full of fruit pies were cooling, and things seemed to be running smoothly.

Sam took a moment to text Kelly: Checking on Riki. How'd it go last night?

Exactly like you'd think. I'm going over to check on her soon.

Sam sighed, feeling for their friend, especially now that she knew Evan's reason for leaving. Which reminded her that it was midmorning, and she wondered what Beau had decided about taking back his old job and whether he'd yet told the mayor.

She surveyed the kitchen, pleased that everything seemed under control. Julio and Becky were a fantastic team, and she reminded herself that with the craziness of the holidays, she wanted to see that they got nice bonuses.

"What time am I supposed to deliver the pies to the festival?" she asked.

"I think they said any time after one o'clock," Becky responded, her attention focused on weaving a lattice crust.

Sam glanced up at the clock on the wall. "Okay, there's a little time. I'm going to touch base with Beau."

She hadn't told anyone about the job offer, not until his decision was made. She pulled her outdoor jacket from its hook and stepped out into the warm November sunshine, taking her phone from her pocket.

"Hey, so what's the verdict?" she asked.

He knew immediately what she was referring to. "I'm leaving the station now. Just wanted to be sure I wasn't stepping on toes if I took the job away from somebody here who might want it more."

"And?"

"Nope, no toes are being harmed. Lawson is senior, and he definitely doesn't want it. Says he's putting in for his retirement in a few months. Rico would be next on the ladder, and he swears he is absolutely happy being a deputy. Hates the idea of ever being the boss."

"And there's no one else in line?"

"Three younger guys, two of whom are really new. They don't have the experience."

"So, you're taking it."

"Looks that way. I'm driving over to the mayor's office now to discuss it all."

"Well, congratulations, Sheriff Cardwell. I'm happy for you."

"You sure? Remember the long hours and sometimes crazy schedule. I want you to be on board with the decision too, Sam."

"I am. Totally." She had seen how much he lit up when he was working this recent case in Oklahoma, how he'd lapped up the respect from younger lawmen. He loved ranching, but he loved this more. There would always be time to tend horses and mend broken fences. Law enforcement was in his blood. And if it sometimes scared the bejeezus out of Sam, she had to support his choice.

She walked back into Sweet's Sweets, taking a few minutes to greet customers and top off coffee mugs. The early rush had settled into the midmorning routine where retirees settled in for coffee and talk. Jen was busy rearranging the display cases, filling gaps where products had sold, showcasing the lunch favorites—quiches and the meat pies Julio probably had in the oven right now.

From the corner of her eye, she spotted Kelly's car pulling up in front of Puppy Chic—Riki's grooming salon next door. Both of the younger women got out, and Sam excused herself from the bakery to go and bestow hugs. Kelly's curly cinnamon-shaded hair looked freshly washed and fluffed, while Riki had opted to pull her long, dark tresses into a neat bun, forego makeup, and leave it at that.

Riki wore dark glasses against the glare of full sun, but she had a smile on her face. Considering the things Kelly had told her about Riki's recent moodiness and temper outbursts, Sam felt a surge of happiness.

"Let's get inside, if you don't mind," Riki said, "Sorry, my head is a bit fragile this morning."

She unlocked the door to her business and they stepped into the lobby, which smelled of scented shampoos and boasted displays of rhinestone dog collars, holiday themed sweaters, and cute little hair bows.

"Luckily, Kelly rescheduled all our morning clients. I would not have been ready."

Sam knew she needed to bring up the difficult subject. "We heard that Evan is leaving town."

"Yes, the whole state, not only me. He's leaving all of us behind. For Dallas! In fairness, he did ask if I'd accompany him, but seriously—can you see me living in a place like Dallas?"

Riki had grown up in a small English village near Cambridge, settled perfectly into the same sort of small-town life here in Taos, and had built a hugely successful business. No, Sam couldn't see her thriving in a metropolis. She told her so, with a hug.

"It seems I have news too," she said, then proceeded to spill the whole story about the mayor's offer and Beau's acceptance. "I hope there aren't hard feelings about him moving so quickly into Evan's job?"

"Oh, pish. Of course not. We all love Beau." Riki stepped behind the counter, stowed her purse, and took off her jacket. "Now—I'm ready to bathe some dogs this afternoon."

"Would you girls like a muffin or something before you get started?" Sam nodded toward the door, with a meaningful glance toward Kelly.

"Sure. I'll walk over with you to get them. You're busy this week. You don't need to deliver to us."

They were no sooner out of range than Kelly opened up. "It looks like Riki and Evan are splitting for good, and she seems fine with it. They'd been having problems for a couple years now. There was the whole fertility thing, where they wanted a baby but it wasn't happening. I think, truthfully, that Evan wanted it more than she did. But I tried to point out that having a baby doesn't fix an unhappy marriage. She agrees. She's ready to get on with her life while he moves to something new in his."

"Okay, well maybe it will work out fine," Sam agreed. "I get the feeling Evan's leaving is best all around, maybe for Beau, too."

Chapter 4

She left Kelly to choose a few muffins and chat with Jen. In the kitchen, one end of the big worktable was stacked with boxed pies and a few cakes, ready for delivery. Sam mapped out her route and began loading the pastries into her delivery van.

Two birthday cakes and three pies were to be delivered in town, so she got those out of the way first. The venue for the Harvest Feast, she learned, was north of Arroyo Seco, almost to the turnoff for Taos Ski Valley, where an old barn had been renovated and converted to a spacious gathering spot for public events. Now known as the Lone Tree Barn because of the huge single cottonwood that had weathered centuries, the place sat on a large tract of land with ample parking.

When she arrived, the entrance was bustling with

delivery trucks of fresh produce and local farmers with pickups loaded with pumpkins and squashes. She spotted a woman in a bright neon-orange vest who seemed to be directing traffic. Sam recognized her as one of the bookshop's customers and a member of their Chocoholics Unanimous book club.

"I've got pies from the bakery, Eva," Sam told her, as if it wasn't obvious by the dramatic artwork on her delivery van.

"Second service entrance on the right. That's the main kitchen." Eva set a forearm on Sam's open window. "The chefs are using the first entrance to access their booths and mini-kitchens."

Sam wasn't sure what that meant but felt sure she would soon find out. She followed a refrigerated truck from Cisneros Farms, the local poultry producer. When he backed up, tailgate to the door, she did the same.

She was vaguely aware of the layout of the venue; she and Beau had attended a dinner dance here shortly after the renovation was completed. The main entrance, large double doors at one end of the old barn, led into a huge open space. Along the back, a kitchen filled most of the space, a room equipped with a professional range, extra ovens, and several refrigerators. But, from what Eva said and what Sam had heard already, the visiting chefs would each have his or her own space in a booth-like mini kitchen, so they could prepare and serve their specialties, receiving proper credit, of course. Sam assumed these facilities would line the side walls of the main room.

Benny Cisneros greeted her as he began to wheel a pallet of boxed, dressed turkeys through the delivery doorway. Sam stacked several pie boxes and followed him into the melee. A frazzled woman seemed a little out of her element in trying to get suppliers to stack their products according to a hand-drawn floor plan.

Sam gave her a sympathetic smile and asked where the pies should go. "I have six more out in my van."

"Um, Nancy's list doesn't mention desserts," the woman said with a nervous glance toward the countertops that already seemed disorganized. "Maybe one of the fridges?"

"They're pumpkin, so yes, they should be refrigerated. Don't worry, I'll find a spot."

She managed to arrange the fridge more logically, with produce in bins, dairy products on the doors, and the pies toward the back of an upper shelf since, presumably, they'd be among the last items to be pulled out. By the time she'd fitted all twelve of them in, the flow of delivery traffic outside had dwindled. She moved her van to the parking lot and decided to take a quick peek inside the main room to see how things were going.

As expected, the entire center of the big space was filled with long tables and benches. Two teens were rolling out long sheets of white paper over the tables and taping it in place. A woman with a cart laden with small centerpieces of chrysanthemums, asters, and tiny pumpkins followed along, setting the bright little arrangements on the tables at intervals. Sam smiled. It looked like Thursday's feast for the less fortunate would strike a tone of bounty and cheer.

She saw six of the little mini-kitchens, three along each long wall of the rectangular building. Each had a banner above it with the name of the sponsoring restaurant: Casa de Rodriguez, Piñon Tree Lodge, Taos Bits and Bites, The Savory Duck, Farmer's Table, and Big Range Cookin'. Several of the places were bustling with activity as the chefs and their assistants began to set up. From what Becky had told Sam, these were mainly to be part of the Friday and Saturday festivities.

The traditional Thanksgiving dinner would be prepared and served from the big kitchen in back, and it was intended for those who might not have the resources for such a large meal at home. But for the rest of the weekend, the focus would be on activities and food for anyone who wanted to attend.

One particular draw was the theme of "Leftovers—How to Make Them Shine!" where chefs would share their recipes and prepare samples to spiff up the inevitable leftover turkey, dressing, cranberries, veggies, and desserts. Could they possibly come up with any better alternative to green bean casserole? She smiled at the thought.

"Nando! What the hell!" Raised voices from the booth nearest the kitchen caught her attention. "Your crate of tortillas is in my booth."

Sam—and nearly everyone in the room—turned to catch sight of the celebrity chef, Hernando Rodriguez. Nando Rodriguez was in his sixties, with graying hair and a stocky build, dressed in his kitchen whites, even though this was only supposed to be the setup day. His signature white chef's hat slumped softly on his head. His jowly face, always lit with a smile on television, sent a ferocious glance toward the complainer.

Sam recognized Nancy Whitson, the event organizer, whose chin-length bob seemed to have received a fresh application of sable brown Miss Clairol in recent days. She'd rushed over to placate both chefs. Sam had edged closer, curious about what type of dish the famed chef would be presenting, and now she picked up the undertones in the conversation.

"Just because he's famous and we're not, it doesn't

mean he can take over the whole place."

"Mr. Jennings, don't worry. There's bound to be a little clutter until everyone gets organized." The organizer's wide smile didn't work on the chef from Santa Fe's renowned Piñon Tree Lodge. She turned to Rodriguez and pursed her mouth. "Nando, can we work with others a bit?"

Nancy looped an arm through his and led him away from Jennings, almost bumping into Sam.

"We gave you top billing, as you wanted. Please do *not* cause a scene." The words came out through gritted teeth, a whisper that reminded Sam of a mother chastising an errant child.

Interesting. Wasn't Nancy afraid she would run off her top celebrity and lose the whole impact of the event?

"I am preparing one of my signature dishes today, gratis, to share with the other vendors. Isn't that friendly enough?" His voice came out as a growl.

"Nando, I'm just saying …" At that moment the organizer seemed to notice Sam, and she lowered her voice while edging away.

"Don't mind him." A female voice behind Sam startled her. "He's like this. Always."

"I'm so sorry. I didn't mean to eavesdrop. I happened to be standing—"

"Really, no worries. I'm Josie Rodriguez." The woman with the long, dark braid held out her hand.

"Oh—you're his wife?"

"Sister." Josie rolled her eyes upward. "He can't seem to keep a wife around, even though he's tried four times. He chalks it up to being a creative personality. Frankly, he's reaching that point where he's really insecure about competition. His age, you know. Younger and flashier chefs are coming along, like Rory. I try to tell Nando that everyone has their season, their time in the limelight won't last forever. He can't stand that idea."

Sam noted Josie's white jacket. "And you work with him?"

"Sous chef. As the old song goes, I can do anything he can do …"

"Better!" The two of them laughed.

Josie looked up to see Nando returning, a scowl on his face. "Um, I'd better get back to it. He's making turkey taquitos as a snack this afternoon. On Friday, they'll be a part of the food tasting experience."

"Josie! What the hell are you doing out here? Is the red chile compote ready?" He looked ready to burst a blood vessel so Sam scurried out of the way.

In the adjacent booth, Rory Jennings had shoved the case of corn tortillas across to Nando's booth and turned back to organizing his own kitchen space. Canisters and packets of spices lined his back counter, while his saucepans and knives were set up beside the cutting board and built-in electric range top.

Sam wandered to the other side of the big indoor space. Here, too, a couple of the chefs were present, preparing what appeared to be snacks, perhaps for the volunteers who'd worked all day to set up the festival. She caught the scents of green chile, tortilla chips, and grilled chicken. One had created fancy spirals of tortilla with fillings that looked like a mix of cranberries and nuts. It was only a preview of the goodies that were to come later in the week.

She was near the main entrance, ready to head back to her van, when she heard the scream.

"*Nando!* Help, someone! Call 911!"

Sam spun toward the commotion. A small crowd had gathered around the Casa de Rodriguez booth, several with their cell phones out.

"Is he choking?"

"Help him!"

As Sam approached the workstation, the shouts halted into an eerie silence, and the voices became sobs. The famed chef was dead.

Chapter 5

Beau appeared in the doorway. Despite the tragedy in the room, Sam's first thought was how handsome he looked in uniform. The day they met, she'd been at the scene of a sudden death, and he had come. Her heart still fluttered when she saw him.

EMTs rushed to the victim. Beau caught sight of her and approached, while two of his deputies fanned out. In as few words as possible, Sam told him the little she knew. "I was halfway across the room when it happened. The woman with the dark braid and the white jacket is his sister. And you know Nancy Whitson, head of the chamber of commerce. The two of them, and the booth holder next to that one, are the only people I saw talking with him. But I haven't been here long."

"If it's true that he's deceased, we'll have to get an autopsy."

"Someone shouted that he was choking. Maybe it was accidental?"

"Still need the autopsy." He pulled out his phone and placed a call to the OMI, the medical investigator, and gave a rundown of the circumstances. "Any chance to get this done overnight? There's a pretty big event going on here and we need answers ASAP."

He listened, ended the call, and turned to Sam. "Who would have guessed that the best time to die is right before a holiday. They'll rush it through so everyone in their office can have a couple days off."

"How can I help?" Sam asked, suddenly feeling like she was in the way.

"We'll need names and contact details for everyone who's here. In case questions come up." He tilted his Stetson back and surveyed the room. "I really can't see bringing several dozen people into my station right now."

He and Sam stepped over to the center of the action, where deputies had asked the onlookers to move aside. One of the EMTs turned to Beau. "From the color of his face, tongue, and fingernails, I'm guessing there's a poison of some kind involved."

"Damn. Not good news in a place where food is about to be served to a crowd."

Chapter 6

Sam felt dead on her feet as she handed over her list of names and numbers to Beau. They'd herded everyone away from the kitchen and cook-stations, dividing the crowd into three groups. Rico had covered one third, Lawson another, and Sam the rest. People had been surprisingly cooperative, including the visiting chefs, who unanimously wanted their kitchens inspected before any food was prepared and served. No one wanted to take the risk of getting a tainted-food reputation. A team from the Department of Health was on the way.

Nancy Whitson was in the worst shape, alternating between stunned silence and wailing over the fact that the event she'd been planning for months was coming to such an early and unsavory end. Her reputation and that of Taos would be ruined. One of the volunteers from the main kitchen stayed with her, trying to calm her down.

"Go home and get some rest," Beau told Sam. "I don't know what time you got up this morning but it was too early."

"Way too early," she agreed. "I'll return the bakery van and switch it for my truck. Are you coming home soon?"

He sighed. "Most likely not."

The next time she saw him was when she dropped by the sheriff's department with two Cobb salads from their favorite restaurant.

"We ate way too much fast food during our trip. Tonight, we're going healthy." She set the bag on his desk and turned around to take in his old office. "Lot of memories here. How does it feel being back?"

He leaned back in his chair, nodding. "Good. It feels good."

Sam pulled out the chilled salads, little tubs of dressing, and forks. "I bet the guys are happy to have you back. They missed you."

"So they say." He dribbled lemon-Dijon dressing over the greens, stirred everything together, and took a big bite.

"Well, they told me they did. Rico said Evan was okay, but he was always haggling for more money to buy new equipment and such."

"Nothing wrong with updating our way of doing things."

"I got the sense the arguments and bargaining was the fun part for Evan."

Beau shrugged. "Maybe he belonged in a big-city department all along."

Sam stabbed half a cherry tomato with her fork, savoring the tartness when she bit into it. "Any further word about that chef who died?"

"I talked to Milt at the OMI's office in Albuquerque. They delivered the body a little while ago. He plans to do the autopsy tonight and get back to me. It'll take several hours, so I'll head home once I organize the lists of people we need to question."

"I can help if you like," she offered. "The bakery's busy, but most of our sales will happen tomorrow. Thursday, we're closed for the holiday."

"It could be helpful to have some extra hands on deck. I really need most of the guys out in their cruisers. Big holiday weekend, and there'll be the usual drinkers and traffic infractions. Plus, there's snow in the forecast. Only a twenty percent chance, but still."

"I'll plan to get up early in the morning to handle my bakery duties, then I'll check in with you."

His desk phone rang and the dispatcher informed him Nancy Whitson was on the line. He rolled his eyes and picked it up. "Hello, Mrs. Whitson, what can I do for you?"

Sam caught herself yawning as she cleared away the empty salad bowls. Her early morning was catching up with her, and if there was to be another of those tomorrow, she had to get some sleep. She picked up her jacket and blew him a kiss. He grinned at her past the chittering voice that was coming over the phone line.

An hour later, Sam stirred in her sleep when Beau walked toward their bathroom. "Everything okay?" she murmured.

"As okay as it can be." He wiped toothpaste from his face and came into the bedroom to undress. "Nancy Whitson is all in a dither over whether to cancel the event or go ahead and try to keep the problem hushed up. Seems most of the vendors want to keep it quiet. They swear they did nothing wrong and all that food will go to waste."

Sam plumped her pillow and rolled to her side. "What do you think?"

"We need to keep investigating. We can't take chances with the public health. This whole thing could quickly turn into a disaster." He leaned over and gave her a kiss. "Go back to sleep. I'll probably read for a little while."

She'd set her alarm for four o'clock but actually woke up fifteen minutes early. As quietly as possible, she showered and dressed, carrying the carved wooden box downstairs with her. The dogs, in their beds near the fireplace, barely lifted their heads as she packed the box into her pack and pulled on her jacket.

The black sky showed a vivid array of stars, and Sam breathed the cold, crisp air. A light dusting of snow had fallen overnight, the kind that would be gone the moment the sun came out. While her truck warmed up, she pulled out the box and held the lumpy surface between her hands. The energy it sent into her arms and shoulders would serve her well this morning.

By six o'clock when Julio walked into the bakery, Sam had half of the day's pie orders done. Julio didn't comment but went directly to his normal morning routine, mixing batter for muffins, cutting scones and putting them into the bake oven.

"Becky's gonna love you," he said, pausing when Sam brought him a mug of coffee. "Her kids have a short day."

Sam smiled at the memories of the days when Kelly was in school and she'd had to adjust her work schedule accordingly.

"I promised Beau I'd lend a hand out at the festival if I

could break away from here. He's got dozens of witnesses to question and the holiday has left the department short-staffed."

Becky walked in as she was speaking, stared at the laden worktable, and smiled. "Well, I'd say we're in good shape here. I don't know how you do it, but I'm not complaining."

Out front in the sales area, Sam heard the door bells tinkle and the sounds of Jen greeting the first customers of the day. She excused herself to call Beau.

"Oh yeah, I'm up," he said when he picked up on the second ring. "Just spoke with Milt on the autopsy results, so I'm heading for the office early."

"What did he say?"

"Rodriguez definitely died from a toxin. The good news is that it wasn't any of the foodborne types—not E.coli or salmonella or anything like that. The bad news is that this chemical toxin had to have been deliberately put into something the victim ate. It's murder."

"Oh, Beau." Sam envisioned the dozens of people milling about in the old barn yesterday. "There are so many suspects."

"Right. We need to question all of them, and we've got to get all the food inspected, to be sure this wasn't more than a personal attack on Rodriguez. There's a lot of food in that building and someone could have tainted a big enough supply of it to kill off half the town."

Her stomach did a flip-flop. "I'll come out and help. We've got things under control here at the bakery."

"Thanks. I appreciate it."

Sam's mind whirled with the possibilities. Could this be some kind of terror attack or attempt at mass murder in the tiny town of Taos?

* * *

Sam arrived at the festival venue to find the parking lot crowded with law enforcement vehicles, plus four with NM Department of Health insignia on their doors. One of their officers met her at the entrance and required her to empty her bag and pockets for inspection.

"Sorry, but we can't take the chance that any new substances are introduced in here until we find the cause of the problem."

Sam assured the woman she understood, but privately she thought it was a case of locking the barn door, so to speak, after the horse was gone. Surely, whoever had brought a killer toxin into the building had taken the container away yesterday and would not be bringing more. But she didn't say so.

Now inside, she glanced around. Health inspection teams had roped off all the kitchenette booths and the main kitchen in the building. Vendors were being guided to the back of the building, where Beau and his deputies had set themselves up at tables, widely apart, so questioning could be done discreetly. Beau caught her eye and motioned her over, stepping away from his interview with Rory Jennings, the chef from the booth next to Nando's.

"So, let me know what to do," Sam offered.

"Interviews. We've got all the chefs and their helpers here, and everyone's anxious about their booths. As the health department clears each one, we can let the staff go back to their places, but until then we're trying to see what we can learn." He reached into his shirt pocket. "Here's a short list of the basic questions: Where were they right before Rodriguez got sick, did they have words with him or know of anyone who did, can they think of any reason someone hated the victim … that kind of thing. See what they say and where the conversation leads after that."

Sam nodded, scanning the list.

"Here's a notepad and pen." Beau picked up the items from the end of the table where they were standing. "You can take that table over there. Want to start by talking to Lucy Garcia from Taos Bits and Bites?"

"Sure. I know Lucy—not well—but she'd be a good warm-up for me."

Sam spotted the twenty-something who was standing with two other young women about her age, nervously glancing around the large room. She approached and invited them to her table.

"Well, of course, everyone knows who Nando Rodriguez is … was." Lucy swallowed and took a breath. "I never met him personally but I was hoping to. I mean, he's kind of a hero to anyone who wants to become a serious chef." The others nodded, their faces somber.

At Sam's second question, one of Lucy's assistants spoke up. "Yesterday, I overheard the guy from the booth next to his. He kind of raised his voice about something."

"Do you know what the argument was about?" Sam knew, but this was a test of the strength of the rumor mill.

The girl shook her head. "Not really. I picked up on the word 'tortillas.' I guess that's silly. Half of us in here are using tortillas in some way."

"Did any of you approach the Casa de Rodriguez booth, maybe to ask a question or anything? Did you speak to anyone there?"

Heads shook, all around.

"Have you heard any gossip, anything that would tell us who might have been out to get Nando?"

Lucy started to say no, but then she paused. "In the booth next to ours, a couple was saying something about the Rodriguez's business. Let me think … something about them having financial troubles. I don't know if it means anything at all. It was such a quick comment and I might have misunderstood."

"No, that's fine," Sam told her, jotting a note. "Anything might turn out to be helpful. We'll check it out." She glanced up, noting that Lucy's booth was next to one called The Savory Duck.

"Can you think of anything else that might be helpful for either the health inspectors or the sheriff's department to know?" She turned to her notes, giving them a moment to think, but no one spoke up.

"If you remember something else, anything at all, please call this number and give the information. The sooner we can figure out what happened here, the sooner everyone gets back in business, okay?"

She handed each of the three young women one of the sheriff department's business cards, a reminder that Beau needed to get his own printed again soon. Or not. He was, after all, only in the job temporarily.

The couple who owned The Savory Duck in Santa Fe were up next on Sam's list and she called them over. Chelsea and Aaron Finsted appeared very much an up-and-coming couple in their late thirties, sharply dressed, exuding confidence and reflecting the contemporary vibe of their logo and their booth. Their restaurant was reputed to be one of the most upscale in the northern part of the state, and they'd made no secret that they planned to branch out to Breckenridge and Scottsdale in the coming years.

"Personal encounter with Nando Rodriguez?" Aaron's expression turned sour. "Not if I can help it. We both attended the Iron Chef cookoff in Vegas last year, and the man was rude beyond belief."

Chelsea nodded. "Yeah, you'd think two chefs from New Mexico would at least pretend to have something in common, a little camaraderie? But no."

"I, personally, was happy to see that our booths were on opposite sides of the room when we got here. I kind of pitied Rory for getting stuck next to Nando."

"We understand the two of them had words yesterday …" Sam left the question dangling.

Chelsea gave a wry chuckle. "Yeah. I saw that. Lucky Rory that it didn't go further."

"Like, getting physical? Was Nando known for that kind of thing?" Sam's pen was poised to take notes.

"Maybe in his younger years," Aaron said. "I don't think he realized his glory days had come and gone."

"Someone mentioned financial trouble?"

"That's the rumor. Supposedly Nando developed a taste for the casinos."

Chelsea tapped her husband's shoulder. "Well, yeah, we saw that in Vegas for ourselves." She faced Sam. "Those high-roller tables for blackjack? Yeah boy, we saw old Nando there nearly every night after the chef competition was done."

Interesting. Sam wondered if Beau was getting similar stories from his interviews.

"One more thing," she posed to the gossipy couple. "Can you think of anyone who would have gone so far as to kill him?"

Aaron made a *pffft* sound. "Who wouldn't?"

Chelsea stiffened. "Careful, honey." She turned to Sam with earnest eyes. "Listen, I can't say that I know anyone who actually *liked* him, but going so far as to kill him—no. That takes a lot of …"

"Moxie?" Aaron had calmed down a little. "Yeah, Chels is right. Just because you don't like someone, you don't plot to kill him. Well, *we* don't."

They'd covered their bases nicely, Sam thought as she handed them a card and gave the usual advice to call if they thought of anything else pertaining to the case. Still, there was a lot of anger and professional jealousy lingering with these two.

Chapter 7

Sam looked across the room, noticing that Beau was free at the moment. She strolled over to him.

"I think we've covered all the booth holders and those working directly with them," he told her. "Lawson has been interviewing the volunteers in the main kitchen. We should put our heads together and see what information has come out."

Sam glanced around at the health inspectors, who were still busily at work, going through trash cans and swabbing surfaces in the little kitchens. "I could go for some coffee right now, but I doubt we should consume anything prepared in this building until those guys have given the all-clear."

"Right. Let's get our team together. We'll find someplace where we can compare notes."

They settled on a diner on the north end of Taos, where the breakfast crowd had dissipated and the lunch bunch hadn't begun to gather. The coffee wasn't nearly as good as what Sam served at Sweet's Sweets, but sometimes you went with what was most convenient.

A few minutes were consumed with choosing seats at a tucked-away corner table, ordering coffees all around, doctoring their beverages with varying amounts of cream and sugar, and settling in.

"Lawson, how about if you go first? Give us the rundown on what you discovered in the main kitchen."

"Sure, Sheriff." The older deputy pulled out his notebook. "I spoke with twelve volunteers who had been tasked with organizing the food deliveries yesterday. Today, they were supposed to begin preparing the side dishes. They told me there were so many turkeys to roast that most of them planned to take one home and cook it in their own ovens, as the Lone Tree Barn's kitchen didn't have enough space."

He cleared his throat and took a sip of his coffee. "That's background information. I asked if any of them had interactions with the deceased. Two admitted to having met him on previous occasions. The others all said no. All agreed that Hernando Rodriguez had not set foot in the main kitchen at all yesterday. Apparently, his food orders were delivered directly to his booth, or he brought everything with him."

"The two workers who had met him … Did they give you more details? Any comments on how well they knew him or what their feelings were about him?"

"I got the feeling they were sort of … I don't know … chef groupies or something. Both women said they'd seen him on some TV show and wanted to meet him. When I pressed for details, both admitted they'd introduced themselves and the victim had barely said hello."

"Feeling snubbed could provide a motive, maybe?" Sam suggested.

"Anything's possible," Lawson admitted. "But these were real grandmotherly types, gray-haired churchy ladies. If that makes sense."

"Anyone stand out as a possible suspect for this?" Beau asked.

Lawson shook his head. "Not really. Two women from the health department were working in there, and they said the kitchen was spotless—not a trace of anything suspicious."

Beau sighed. "Okay, we can probably rule out the main kitchen. What did we learn from the participating vendors? Rico?"

The younger deputy pulled out his notes. "I spoke with Ricky Serna and Bobby Chavez from The Farmer's Table in Española. I grew up down the road from their place and knew their families since I was a kid, so we got to reminiscing about our school days and all."

"Not to the point of being distracted from the important questions, I hope."

Rick shook his head. "Not at all. That was the warmup, leading them to share gossip if they had any."

"And did they?"

"Some. Rumor around the Española Valley is that, in their words, 'the hotshot chef from Albuquerque had money troubles,' and that Nando had been scrambling to find investors to help bail him out."

Beau's gaze sharpened. "Yeah, I got something similar

from the owners of Big Range Cookin' out of Albuquerque. The part about Rodriguez being on the search for investors, I mean."

Sam related what she'd learned from Chelsea and Aaron Finsted, about Nando's gambling habit. "It sounds like money definitely plays into this somehow. Maybe a financial background check, to see if he owed money to bad enough people who'd want to get rid of him?"

Beau jotted notes about the various comments on the victim's finances. "What else?"

Rico shook his head. "That's about all I got."

Sam shared the rest of the interviews she'd conducted, including the obvious professional jealousy on the part of the Finsted couple.

"I heard one other tidbit," Beau said, "but I'm suspecting it could just be juicy gossip." He turned to Sam. "A woman might be able to get more details on this, but what was hinted to me was that Rodriguez might have been carrying on with a married woman. The folks from Big Range said they didn't know who it was, but they suspected someone outside Albuquerque. Nando is so well-known there, if he was trying to hide an affair, he'd need to be careful."

"But he's not married, is he? Someone mentioned he had multiple exes. So, they'd be trying to hide from her spouse … interesting. But, I suppose it could literally be anyone."

"I'd say the field of suspects is wide open at this point," Beau said, closing his notebook. "It seems the man was not well liked, and we've now got several potential motives."

"So, what next, boss?" Lawson shifted in his seat. "The folks working in the kitchen really need to know if they're still cooking for a crowd or not. And that organizer lady … Nancy something. She's having a fit. I never saw such an emotional wreck over a dinner."

Sam nodded. "A meal like Thanksgiving dinner doesn't *happen* to come together at the last minute. Everyone's uncertainty is understandable."

Beau stood up. "I need to get back out there and see what the health department is doing. They promised to do their best to be both thorough and quick. If they decide to shut down the whole event, well, I may have a crowd control situation on my hands. Rico, you're with me."

Lawson muttered something about how he was supposed to have been on patrol this morning, so he left to check in with dispatch.

Sam walked out to Beau's cruiser with him, intending to ride back to the Lone Tree Barn and either help him or to retrieve her own vehicle and get back to the bakery. "I haven't seen Josie Rodriguez around this morning," she said, buckling her seatbelt.

"I talked with her right after the medics took her brother's body away yesterday. She was pretty shaken up. Said she'd be back to pack up their kitchen gear after she went to Albuquerque to be with the rest of the family."

"I imagine everything's really up in the air for them. Not going to be a good holiday, is it?"

"Doesn't look that way. I suppose I should make some inquiries, find out when the funeral will be."

"Would you attend?"

"Might not be a bad idea. If we don't come up with a solid suspect pretty soon, I probably should drive down there, assuming it will be in Albuquerque. It's not unheard of for killers to attend their victim's funeral, some weird kind of closure, I suppose."

Back inside the Lone Tree, Sam saw that the plastic quarantine tape the health department folks had stretched everywhere was now gone from the main kitchen door and several of the booths. The leader of that team, a stern looking woman in her forties, approached Beau.

"We've cleared the kitchen and given the go-ahead for them to prepare and serve the big dinner here tomorrow."

"Nancy Whitson will be relieved," Sam said, looking around for the president of the chamber of commerce. "What about the other booths? They were planning on being here Friday and Saturday."

"We're not completely done here, but so far, the only place we found any trace of the toxin was in a half-eaten taco inside the Casa de Rodriguez booth. It must have been the item the victim ate."

"Wow—quick acting poison." Sam felt a little stunned.

"It's nasty stuff. We bagged all edibles from that booth and are turning them over to you, Sheriff. Assuming it will all become part of a criminal case?"

Beau nodded. "Sadly, yes. It's looking that way. What about a container for this toxin? Do we have an idea how it was brought in?"

"We're leaving that to you and your forensics people. Our authority only covers the food. Still, to be safe, we're advising every vendor to throw out all consumables that aren't in hermetically sealed packaging. Safer if they bring in a whole new supply. And every bit of their kitchen equipment should be thoroughly cleaned and sanitized."

Beau nodded and the woman walked away. "Too bad. I'm sure that will be a financial hardship for some of them."

"Better to buy all new food than to risk a tragedy or a lawsuit."

Sam felt her phone vibrate and retrieved it from her pocket. The number was for Puppy Chic.

Chapter 8

Sam took the call as Beau's attention got diverted elsewhere.

"Hey, Mom, I'm at work right now, and Riki and I are discussing Thanksgiving dinner. Even though I'd planned on doing the turkey and bigger things at my house, I'm wondering if Beau's going to be available—you too, for that matter. How are things going with the investigation?"

"I don't know. There are no clear-cut answers at this point, although it does look like they'll be able to serve food out here tomorrow."

"Good. I'm relieved to know that part of it's okay. And so far, we haven't heard anything in the news about any of this." She lowered her voice. "That's why I'm calling between clients here at the shop."

"Thanks. If the rumor mill gets going, it'll mean a lot

of food wasted, food that should be going to people who genuinely need it."

"If anyone says anything to me, all I've heard is that someone died while the event was getting set up. I have no idea how they died or what else has happened."

"Good. We'll keep it at that."

"And so … Riki and I were talking earlier. Can we volunteer to help out? We could help with the cooking, or at least with serving the dinners or something. We both feel like we want to be part of the community effort. If we postpone our family Thanksgiving meal, Beau can make it and we will have contributed to something bigger."

"I think that's a great idea. Figure out who needs to know about the change in plans—there was your family, Beau and me, Riki …"

"Emily from the library, and maybe Rupert." Kelly paused a moment. "That's it. I'll make the calls and tell them we're doing Sunday instead of Thursday. Sound good?"

One less event to deal with by tomorrow—it sounded perfect to her. She made a call to check in at Sweet's Sweets, where Jen assured her everything was going fine. More than half the Thanksgiving orders had already been picked up. Becky and Julio were taking care of a few last-minute things. Sam felt the weight lift from her shoulders.

Sam looked around the Lone Tree Barn, taking in the activity at the various booths. There seemed to be a little grumbling among the vendors, but most were happy to be back on track to continue their work. Beau walked over to her.

"I called in Lisa. Once she arrives to go through everything in the Rodriguez kitchenette, I'll be free for other things. I want to run by the hotel where Nando was staying, see what was left behind in the room." He jammed his small notebook into his shirt pocket. "If you want to ride along, I'll buy lunch when we're done there."

"I could go for some lunch. The smell of roasting turkey from the kitchen is starting to seem pretty appealing."

The female manager at the Arrowhead Lodge went into a bit of a dither when the tall, handsome sheriff showed up in the office.

"Hernando Rodriguez, yes, I recall when he checked in." She clicked a few keys on a keyboard and turned her computer's screen to a better angle. "Let's see, that was Monday evening … Two rooms, next to each other."

"What was the name on the second room?"

"Josie Rodriguez. I believe she said she was his sister. I'm showing that Ms. Rodriguez checked out Tuesday evening. Mr. Rodriguez's room is still active, but I don't see that housekeeping tended to the room today." Her mouth pursed.

"We need access to those rooms, please." Beau kept his tone polite but official.

"Of course. Shall I call to announce you?"

He shook his head. Obviously, the hotel staff had not received word about the death. Which was good—the whole idea had been to keep it quiet. The manager handed over two plastic key cards.

The whitewashed adobe lodge consisted of a two-story structure with rooms on three sides of a square, a pool and gathering area in the center, the office and a restaurant on the fourth side, which faced the street. Parking slots circled the building, allowing guests to park within sight of their rooms. Sam and Beau followed the directions to a first-floor room near the back of the property. Room 127 had a

Privacy Please sign hanging from the door handle.

Beau let them in, donning the latex gloves he pulled from his back pocket and handing a pair to Sam. "We need to treat this as part of the crime scene until we know otherwise. Anything in here could be evidence."

They entered to find a standard hotel room, decked out with standard New Mexico décor—a woven dreamcatcher above the bed, enlarged photographs of Taos Pueblo and the Rio Grande Gorge, faux-Indian patterned drapes.

Unfortunately, there wasn't much to find. The bed had been left in untidy disarray, but no luggage or toiletries had been left behind, no clothing in the closet niche.

Beau leaned into the bathroom and stepped back out. "Josie must have come in and taken his stuff home when she went back to Albuquerque."

"Looks like he shared the bed with someone. Both pillows have head-dents in them and the covers are all over the place." Sam met Beau's eyes. "Ew, surely not his sister."

"She had her own room. Which is probably why Nando felt safe enough having someone else visit."

"The mysterious affair?"

"Maybe. Let's bag the bedding, in case forensic needs to test anything." He walked back to his truck to get supplies.

While he was gone, Sam pulled open the nightstand drawer and turned on the lamp to check around the edges of the king-size bed. She found a hair clip—one of those little butterfly types used to hold back a half-up style—and a button. The clip was so generic it would be hard to say where it came from or who dropped it. The button was unusual, silver, probably Indian made. She guessed Zuni or Hopi. It was substantial in weight, probably came from a jacket.

Touching it only on the edges, she showed it to Beau, then dropped it into the small plastic evidence bag he held open.

Across the room, a small refrigerator revealed nothing; same with the microwave on top of it. But peeking from beneath the micro, Sam spotted the corner of a paper. When she pulled it out, she discovered it was a brochure for the nearby Taos Mountain Casino.

"A clue?" she asked, holding it up for Beau to see.

"We heard he liked to gamble. Probably worth a drive out there to ask a few questions."

While he stripped the bedding, placed everything in an evidence bag, and wrote up a receipt for the hotel, Sam walked over to the adjacent room Josie had occupied. It had the freshly cleaned scent and professionally made bed that told her the housekeeping staff had already done their thing. She did a quick walk-through, found nothing, and closed the door behind her.

They popped in at the office to return the keys and inform the manager they had removed a set of sheets from number 127.

"Well, I'm not sure we learned anything at all there, other than an educated guess that Nando spent the last night of his life with someone." Sam buckled her seatbelt while he started the truck.

"Cases have been solved on exactly that kind of evidence," he commented. "The biggest challenge we'll have here is that any DNA that might be connected to the room will have to come from someone who's already in a database. And among average citizens, that's fairly rare. Still, with the gambling connection, Nando could have gotten himself in trouble with somebody who's not one of your average citizens. We can't rule it out."

Ten minutes later, they pulled into the parking lot of the Taos Mountain Casino. This early in the day, the place wasn't exactly booming and they quickly found the manager talking to a pretty, young cashier in the booth.

"Hey, Sheriff, I thought I heard you'd retired." The Tiwa man stepped out and shook Beau's hand, giving Sam a smile of recognition.

"Leroy, good to see you again. Yeah, it kind of looks like I'm un-retired now, at least for a while." He pulled out a photo of Hernando Rodriguez, clipped from one of the festival brochures. "I need to know if this man came in Monday night."

"Sure, boss, let's check." Leroy led the way to an Employees Only door, which he unlocked with a key on a springy cord around his wrist. "Gotta find out who was on duty. Any idea what time?"

"They checked into their room about five p.m.," Sam said, remembering a comment from the manager at the Arrowhead Lodge. "Had to be after that."

"And we close at ten." Leroy grinned at them. "This isn't Vegas, you know."

"Nothing in Taos is, thank goodness." Beau studied the small office, where two video monitors covered the casino floor and table games. "Hey, maybe you have film from then?"

"Monday? Nope, we erase and tape over every twenty-four hours. Unless we catch someone cheating at the games. In that case we'd keep the evidence until they're prosecuted. But, man, that's so rare here. We're a little place, mostly a family hangout. The last time I remember catching a cheater, it was a guy reaching over to palm chips from the blackjack dealer's table. We confronted him and he gave them back when we threatened to tell his grandmother, up at the pueblo. We banned him for six months and he's been clean ever since. That's the kind of place we run."

Beau nodded.

"Okay, here we go. Benny was here that night, Benny Yazzie. He's coming in for his next shift in about an hour. Maybe you want to have some lunch while you wait?"

A blatant hint to buy something here, and why not? Sam followed Beau toward the snack bar, where for less than five dollars each they filled up on taquitos and chicken wings. She was wiping sauce from her fingers when she looked up to see a man approaching them.

Benny Yazzie was probably in his late forties, a little on the stocky side, with a round friendly face. "Sheriff Beau! Good to see you again."

Beau gestured for Benny to join them and asked if he'd like them to get more taquitos.

"Nah, I'm good. Leroy says you were asking about a customer who was here a few days ago?"

They went through the routine of showing Nando's photo, waiting while Benny studied it. "Yeah, I've seen him. He wouldn't have been wearing this chef hat, right?"

Sam smiled. "No, no chef hat. But you may have seen him on television if you watch cooking shows."

Benny shook his head. "Nope, not me. The wife likes to watch those, but thank goodness she doesn't get fancy with her cooking. I like my usual breakfast burrito, that's it."

"He may have hit the blackjack tables. We got the impression he's not a slot machine kind of guy."

"Yeah, yeah, I seem to remember he won some, not a

lot but better than break-even."

"Did he come in alone, leave alone?"

"Interesting you ask it that way. I'd say yes, and no. Came in by himself around six, maybe seven. Played a couple hours. A woman joined him at some point. She was kind of dressed up, but not like all glamorous or anything. Just stylish. Black pants and a clingy top."

"Did it seem like they knew each other already? Or did you get the impression it was a random hookup?"

Benny shook his head. "I wouldn't know. I must have been in the other room when she arrived 'cause she was suddenly there. Definitely romantic though. She kept messing with his collar, running her finger along his jaw."

"Did that bother him?"

"Didn't take his mind off the game, for sure. But it could account for them leaving before closing."

"Can you tell us what she looked like?"

"Anglo. He's Latino, right? Neither of them were Tiwa, that's for sure."

"Anything more specific?"

"Probably about the same age as him, brown hair about to here." He indicated his chin. "Nice looking lady, but I didn't notice much else."

Sam had a thought. "Beau, do you have the button we found?"

"In the truck. I'll grab it." He was back in under two minutes and held out the little plastic bag with the silver button in it.

"Hm. Nice work. Hopi, I'd guess. It's not made around here."

"Could this button have come from the woman's clothing? Or his, I suppose," Beau asked.

Benny shrugged. "Anything's possible, but I didn't specifically see it on either of them. I can ask the night shift blackjack dealer if she remembers anything. She'll be on duty at six."

They thanked him for the information, handed over a business card, and asked Benny to keep them informed.

"What next?" Sam asked as they walked out to his truck.

"I've got a couple of the guys working on a background check of the victim. Shall we drop in at the office and see if they've come up with anything?"

"I'll check in with Becky and see if I'm needed at the shop."

Sam hit the Sweet's Sweets number as Beau pulled out of the casino parking lot.

"So glad you called, Sam. We've got a little situation here."

Chapter 9

Thanks for coming back over," Becky said when Sam walked into the bakery. "I would have sworn that fabric swatch was stapled to the order form. I remember it being a shade of purple, but this is also a really picky bride, and if her cake flowers don't match the bridesmaids' dresses, she'll know it immediately."

"It's okay, we'll find it. Did you check my desk?"

"I did, but you might look again. I didn't really want to poke around too much."

"Not to worry—it would be fine." Sam started with the top drawer and worked her way down. "When did we take that order, anyway?"

"It had to be late September. I was out for a week, and I'm pretty sure you and Jen met with the bride and her mother. The form is filled out in your writing."

Sam read through the details. Under 'special instructions' was the notation that the sugar-paste flowers must be tinted to match attached fabric sample, and there were two little holes where something had been stapled.

"I love it when people place wedding orders early," Becky said, "but this situation is one of my nightmares."

"Did we see the swatch recently? Maybe last Friday when we organized this week's work?"

"You know … I think I do remember it. Okay, so it hasn't been lost for months, only a few days at most."

They began scanning the shelving units and the floor for the missing square of material. Becky was starting to get shaky when Julio held up a little thing. "Could this be it?"

"Ohmygosh yes! That's it!" Becky patted her chest as she rushed across the kitchen. "Thank you."

"It must have torn loose from the order and drifted to the floor by the cooling racks."

Sam told Becky to breathe again and guaranteed her it wasn't a disaster. Even though it would have been a little embarrassing, they could have requested another one from the client. "Crisis averted. Can I bring you a cup of tea?"

Becky shook her head and began pulling the gel food coloring bottles from the shelves so she could experiment with creating a match. Sam wandered to the sales room, where Jen was wiping down the coffee area; she had the display cases neatly arranged for the afternoon crowd. A dozen or more boxed pies waited on the back counter for customers to pick them up. Assuring herself all was well with the business, she stepped out front and called Beau.

"How's it going?"

"Just starting to go through the background reports.

Looks like some interesting stuff. Everything turn out okay at the bakery?"

"Yes, actually, really great. I was thinking about coming over to see if I could help you."

"Any time."

She heard footsteps on the sidewalk and turned to see someone walking out of Mysterious Happenings, the bookshop next door to the west. Nancy Whitson spotted her and quickened her pace. "Sam, I was about to call your husband. Officially, of course. The radio station is waiting on my go-ahead to ramp up the ad campaign for the Friday and Saturday activities at the Harvest Feast. Can we do that?"

"You really need to check that with Beau." Her eyes landed on something familiar. "He's in his office right now, and I was about to walk over. Want to join me?"

"Oh—well, all right."

The three blocks went quickly, although Sam had a hard time keeping her eyes off Nancy's stylish Indian blanket jacket. The desk officer cleared them through to Beau's office, where Sam stood back to let Nancy walk in ahead of her. While Nancy posed her question about whether the event was cleared to proceed, she closed the door and met Beau's eyes over Nancy's shoulder.

Once he'd assured her that all the booths had been inspected and all but the Rodriguez workstation were given the all-clear, Sam coughed discreetly. "I noticed you're missing a button from your coat, Nancy."

Nancy looked down and touched each of the other two silver buttons.

Beau smiled. He had seen it, too. "Lucky for you, we found the missing one." He pulled the small evidence bag from a drawer.

"Where did you get that?" Nancy's tone wasn't so casual any more.

"Why don't you tell us what you were doing in Hernando Rodriguez's hotel room?"

"Nothing! I stopped by to give him the vendor packet for the festival."

"What time was that?"

"Monday evening. I'd guess it was about seven, seven-thirty."

"Was he there at that time?"

"Of course. He thanked me for the packet and said he was looking forward to the event."

"Except, that's not exactly true," Sam said, edging sideways to block the door. "Nando was at Taos Casino. They have security footage of all the casino areas. You actually joined him there, didn't you?"

"Oh, that's right. I delivered the vendor packet to him there because that's where he said he would be."

"Except that the button was in his room, near the bed."

Nancy blanched, her face now standing out in stark contrast to her dark hair.

"Mrs. Whitson, have a seat," Beau said, indicating the chairs in front of the desk. "We heard the rumors about his having an affair. Believe it or not, we're not out to harm your reputation or wreck your marriage. We have a murder to solve, and we need for you to be truthful with us about what you know."

Nancy crumpled into the chair and raised her hands to her face. "I don't *know* anything, not about his death. It's been so horrible for me, grieving while trying to hide my feelings."

"Had you planned a future with him?" Sam asked, as gently as she could.

Nancy took a deep breath and sat a little straighter. "Nando was brilliant in the kitchen and tender in the bedroom. I hadn't gotten far enough into the situation to know if there would be a future. He could be temperamental and so we had our ups and downs. I wasn't sure whether I wanted to end my marriage and move to Albuquerque. His business and family are there. I love Taos and wanted to stay here. So, for the time being, we grabbed moments when we could."

"What do you know about strychnine?"

"Isn't it a rat poison or something? I don't really know." Her tone was firm, her answer sounded honest. "Sheriff, I want to know, as much as anyone, what happened to him. I would *never* have harmed him, not in a million years."

"Any ideas who would?"

She shook her head. "He didn't openly share information with me. I got little hints that there was financial trouble, probably something to do with his gambling. I have to admit the gambling is another thing that made me cautious about getting too involved with him. I've seen people ruined by it."

Beau nodded. "We'll need to hang onto the button for a while, until we have enough evidence to prove it's not relevant. After that, I'll get it back to you."

"Thank you, Sheriff. And I do appreciate your discretion about the relationship. You'll find that it's not relevant to your case, I assure you."

He nodded, without commenting. Sam shifted aside to let Nancy out of the office. Rico had been about to tap on the door, and Sam asked if he would mind showing their guest how to get to the exit.

As soon as they were out of sight, Sam turned to Beau. "Do you believe what she told us?"

"I think so. We'll do some further checking, but it rings true. And what she said about his debts and financial problems fits with other statements we've received. I have a feeling that's what Rico was about to share."

Deputy Lawson tapped on the open door, interrupting a thought that was trying to form in Sam's head. "We've got the backgrounds done, boss. If you've got some time?"

They gathered at the conference table in the squad room—Rico, Lawson, Garcia, Sam and Beau—to discuss the results of the background checks on the victim. Each of the deputies had taken a different aspect of his life and now were ready to report. Rico took the lead.

"So, it appears the rumors we heard about Rodriguez's gambling habit and related debts are true. I spoke quite a while with a contact of mine at APD and learned that Nando's casino of choice was the Isleta one, on the south side of Albuquerque. He'd kind of run through his limit at Sandia and at Route 66, so Isleta was his current pick. And, according to my contact, there are some nasty loan sharks who target these places. These dudes spot vulnerable players from a distance, chat them up, introduce someone who can 'help them out' but then the victim discovers they're in debt for way more and the interest rate is killing them." He looked around the table. "Those were his words, not mine. He assures me the casino management and the tribes stay *way* distanced from these bad guys. They'll accommodate a player up to the limits of their credit cards, but …" he glanced at Lawson.

The older deputy sat up straighter. "Yeah, so that's

where I came in. A standard credit check showed our victim maxed out on several credit cards, interest charges piling up on him, and no bank in the country willing to loan him more."

Beau nodded. "Okay, so far I'm leaning toward the loan sharks and their enforcers. Banks don't generally get deadly. But—loan sharks don't get paid back when they kill someone either, so it's in their best interests to keep him alive and catch up with him on a winning night to extract their due."

"The poisoning is what bothers me," Sam added. "Those ruffians are more about breaking kneecaps, aren't they?"

Everyone around the table nodded.

Garcia took her turn. "On a personal level, he owned his home, heavily mortgaged with a second and a third, and behind on payments. Apparently, his mother is fairly well off, with a lot of property in Santa Fe, but those have appreciated so much that she doesn't want to sell because of a huge tax liability."

"Do we know if she loans him cash?"

"Maybe now and then. It would be completely off the books, so we aren't sure. But another thing I learned about the mom is that she is, or was, an accountant in her younger years, and she helped set up the restaurant as a business and kept the books for it. Doesn't look like he could pull money from that venture without her finding out, and rumor has it she's pretty religious and totally opposed to gambling."

"Hence, the reason for the loan sharks," Sam suggested.

"Most likely." Beau had jotted a few notes and now looked up from his pad. "Seems our guy had a lot of secrets he needed kept from mama. I'm going to talk to the sister again, see what plans they're making for a funeral. If there's a service planned, I may drive down there to attend and check out who else shows up."

Sam leaned forward. "Kelly and I are going to volunteer at the big Thanksgiving feast out at the Lone Tree Barn tomorrow, so we can keep our eyes open toward the staff and other vendors. I'm still thinking there was a lot of professional jealousy directed at Nando. Here he is, a celebrity chef visiting our little town, maybe bruising other egos along the way. And the way he was killed sounds a lot more personal than loan shark enforcers who hang out around casinos."

"You're right. We can't rule anything out, so it's important to keep all our options open. At some point, there will be clues that make sense. Meanwhile, we have other cases and a whole lot of visitors in the area for the holiday weekend, so everyone keep your eyes and ears open."

At his desk again, Beau called the personal number they'd taken down for Josie Rodriguez right after the death, but there was no answer. He left a voicemail and did the same when the main number at Casa de Rodriguez gave a message saying the restaurant was presently closed. He felt frustrated, but supposed it wasn't unrealistic to expect that with their head chef gone and the family grieving, they would take a break.

"I wonder if poor Josie will be able to keep the place running on her own." Sam handed him the mug of coffee she'd poured from the carafe down the hall.

"My impression is that she's an accomplished chef in her own right," he said, taking a sip. "But I imagine it will be a challenge. The world knows the name Hernando Rodriguez. Hers, not so much."

"Yeah, it'll be tough if—" The ringing phone interrupted Sam's thought.

Beau picked up his desk handset. "Thanks, Dixie." He looked up at Sam. "Speaking of …" He pressed the button for line one. "Hello Josie, thanks for returning my call so quickly."

He inquired about plans for her brother's funeral. Sam waited until they'd finished and Beau turned back to her.

"There will be a small service next Wednesday. There's only her mother and herself now, plus some aunts, uncles, and cousins who may come from out of town. She's hoping to keep it quiet from the press, but they may also have to deal with that."

"I gather she asked how the investigation is going? What did she say when you mentioned the rumors about his debts?"

"Not surprised. Said Nando always loved to gamble, since he was a kid betting on sports games with his buddies on the schoolground. She felt bad for enabling him by not tattling, but said she didn't want her mother to find out, especially now that she's quite elderly and not in great health."

"Oh, that's rough."

"She's planning to drive up here this weekend to pick up the kitchen gear that they left in their booth. Probably a quick up-and-back trip."

Sam nodded. "Maybe while I'm at the Lone Tree tomorrow I can help gather it all up so she only has some boxes to load."

"And, unless we have a big break in the case in the next

couple days, I'll plan to go to Albuquerque for the funeral." He stretched in his chair and looked up at the clock on the wall. "I'm tired—time to head home. Guess I'm not used to having a full-time job yet. What about you?"

"Yeah, me too. Jen said a few more people are stopping by to pick up their holiday orders, then she'll empty the display cases and close up. She's going to bring the rest of our pastries to the dinner tomorrow and we'll donate them."

His yawn caused her to do the same, and she remembered what an early morning it had been. Tomorrow would be no less tiring.

Chapter 10

Sam woke at daylight, despite her best intention of sleeping in a bit longer. She rolled to the edge of the bed, thankful that at least today it wasn't one a.m. Beau was already up, and she hoped he'd slept well. He was right about not being acclimated to his new routine yet. She showered and dressed, assuming her normal bakery attire of black pants and a white top would work for today's duties as well.

Downstairs, she prepared a light breakfast for the two of them. By the time Beau finished his ranch chores, showered and ate, it was time to leave. The Lone Tree Barn was a hive of activity already, with the parking area behind the kitchen jammed. They found a spot off to the side and entered through the kitchen door at the back of the building.

Immediately, the scents of Thanksgiving were upon them—roasting turkey, savory stuffing, rich gravy. One of the volunteers was lifting a huge tray of roasted squash, peppers, and corn from an oven. Beau stepped over to grab potholders and lend his muscle to the endeavor.

Sam asked what they could do and was directed to the main area. "They can probably use some help setting up the steam tables in the serving area," the gray-haired woman told her. "Or making sure the dining tables have everything they need."

"Sure thing." She headed through wide swinging doors where she spotted Kelly and Riki. Around the room, the various chefs were in their booths. Rory Jennings appeared to be focused on organizing his kitchen, while Chelsea and Aaron Finsted had an electric mixer going full speed. Apparently, they were planning to whip up some kind of snack or appetizer for the guests. Sam remembered that was optional for the chefs today. Their main duties would happen Friday and Saturday when the goal was to wow everyone with their culinary skills, hand out freebies, and tempt people to buy their jarred sauces, condiments, and cookbooks.

Sadly, the Rodriguez booth sat empty and dark. Cartons with cookware and utensils that had never been unpacked were stacked in the corners. Beau had said Josie planned to drive to Taos at some point and take it all back home with her. Sam sensed movement and heard Kelly's voice.

"Hey, Mom. Do you know how to work these things?" Her daughter was fiddling with the canned Sterno fuel and hot water trays that would keep the food hot once it was brought from the kitchen.

Sam showed her how basic the procedure was, then

walked over to help Riki who was rolling plastic flatware into large paper napkins. She had a bin filled almost to the top, but apparently the goal was to fill two of them.

"It's going to be quite a crowd, according to Nancy Whitson," Riki said.

Sam wondered how the organizer's attitude would be toward her, after yesterday's little confession session.

"What time do we start serving?" Sam glanced toward the entrance the public would use.

"Nancy said the first buses would be coming from town around eleven-fifteen. Since parking might become a problem, and since a lot of the people we're serving might not even have cars, I guess they have pickup locations at several places. The RTD bus will shuttle people out here and back, pretty much all day."

"Eleven to four is what the posters said." Beau had emerged from the kitchen.

"Hey, Sheriff. You look un-sheriffy this morning," Riki said with a smile toward his plaid shirt and jeans.

"Yeah, I thought it would be easier to mingle without the badge and holster to scare people away." He looked over his shoulder. "The kitchen is becoming a complete madhouse and I felt like I was in the way. What can I do out here?"

"Kelly might want help stacking plates or something." Sam walked with him to a quiet spot. "Were you planning on talking to anyone about the case? Asking questions of the other chefs, or anything like that?"

He shook his head. "Playing it by ear. It's a holiday. Mainly, we should keep our eyes open, make sure nobody tries to pull anything."

"They wouldn't … would they? We felt fairly certain

what happened to Nando was personal, right?"

"Most likely. Still, I'm keeping an eye on the crowd. It would be a tragedy if there's a killer intent on getting at others, too."

Just then, the kitchen doors pushed open and four of the kitchen staff came wheeling in with carts of laden food trays. Sam, Beau, and Kelly rushed to help transfer everything to the serving line, and the lids were no sooner on the big trays of turkey, mashed potatoes, stuffing, veggies, and rolls than the first busload of guests came to the front doors. Sam quickly set out the cold dishes—cranberry sauce and salads. Sliced pies went on a side table as the lineup of folks made their way through the large room.

The rest of the day became a blur of activity, smiles, joyful kids, and grateful adults—a success in every way. Nancy Whitson was buoyant as she saw the last of the guests out at five p.m. Sam felt practically dead on her feet and wished she'd drawn some energy from the wooden box ahead of time.

"Did you actually get a chance to ask questions of the vendors?" she asked Beau as they drove home.

"You didn't hear Rory Jennings almost get into it with Ricky Serna from The Farmer's Table?"

"No … what happened?"

"Young males with egos. Luckily, Rory realized who I was, out of uniform, and reined himself in."

"No indication their battle might have been related to what happened to Nando?"

He shook his head. "Everyone is tired, but this is only the first day. I hope they'll lose their sharp edges before tomorrow, because I understand there's a lot more activity planned. Whether they do or not, I'll be back there and in uniform, so they'd better mind their manners."

Beau was right about everyone being tired. They snacked on cheese and crackers for dinner, watched the end of a football game, and fell into bed as early as a pair of eighty-year-olds.

* * *

When Sam woke after a solid ten hours of sleep, she felt refreshed and hopeful for a breakthrough in the case. She needed to run by the bakery before the Harvest Festival opened at nine, to pick up the cinnamon coated bizcochitos Julio had baked yesterday while the bakery was closed for business. Bless him, she thought. There was no way she would have had the energy.

Speaking of which … she walked into the bathroom and picked up the carved box from the vanity, holding it until her hands were warmed by the glowing golden wood. She took a deep breath and dashed downstairs to find Beau in the kitchen, stirring a skillet of scrambled eggs with chunks of ham mixed in.

"Sorry, I don't know how to make them pretty like omelets. But I figure it's the same ingredients." He sprinkled grated cheese on top and let it melt over the whole concoction. "Have you looked outside?"

Sam peered out the window to find there was an inch of fresh snow. "Whoa—did we know this was coming?"

"Kinda. I'd heard something was moving in, but we crashed before checking the weather report last night." He handed her a plate loaded with eggs and two slices of toast.

They carried their breakfast to the dining table, where

they could look out through French doors, over the snowy pasture. Sam spotted Beau's tracks where he'd already been out to tend the horses.

"It's not that cold out, and the clouds are breaking up. Forecast is for it to clear off by this afternoon." He pulled his phone from his shirt pocket and turned the screen toward her. "See? Forty by noon."

"I wonder what effect that'll have on the festival. I think Nancy had planned on some of the activities taking place outdoors."

"She's lived here long enough to know that you always have a contingency plan at this time of year." He looked at Sam. "Don't worry, I'm sure she does."

They ate in silence as a whoosh of white flakes flew off the roof and landed on the wooden deck in front of them. A half hour later they were out the door, Beau checking in at his office before heading out to the festival. Sam let her van warm up, then followed Beau's tracks down the snowy driveway. He was right; the snowfall hadn't amounted to much and it was already warm enough that the highway was mostly clear.

Julio had baked more than two hundred of the cinnamon coated, anise flavored cookies, a New Mexico tradition for the start of the holiday season. Sam stacked the boxes and assured herself she wasn't needed at the bakery. It would probably be a slow day as everyone in town finished up their Thanksgiving desserts and vowed never to eat sweets again, at least until closer to Christmas. Becky had the wedding cake with the purple flowers—the ceremony was tomorrow afternoon. So, all was well at Sweet's Sweets and she headed out.

The Lone Tree Barn had a whole different vibe today.

Gone were the volunteers crowding the main kitchen. Gone were the long rows of tables and benches where they had fed hundreds yesterday. Somehow, overnight the interior space had been filled in with booths bedecked in holiday spirit.

She spotted Nancy Whitson, who suggested she leave at least half the cookies in the kitchen, out of sight, to be served later. The rest could be taken to the Chamber of Commerce booth, where staffers would hand them out. Next over, a booth from a local business, Warm & Fuzzy, was dispensing hot apple cider into small paper cups, the perfect accompaniment to the cookies.

Sam said hello to Linda Fresquez, the woman who'd come up with the Warm & Fuzzy concept—comforts of all types. The shop was one of Sam's favorites, with its huge selection of mixes for soups and stews, hot beverages such as the cider, and luscious boxed chocolates and decadent nibbles. The other half of the store featured cozy clothing, shawls, blankets, and afghans hand made by local artisans. It was one of the most popular shops on the plaza.

"Hey, Sam," Linda said after they'd hugged, "I saw Beau walking around. I hope there's not some kind of trouble out here?"

The other thing about Linda was that she loved any juicy bit of gossip, and Sam wasn't going there. She didn't mind when Nancy Whitson stepped over and interrupted.

"What are we going to do about the bouncy-pumpkin? We put a picture of it on the posters, and kids are starting to ask. We have a spot for it in the parking lot, but things got kind of messed up by the snow."

"Maybe suggest that it's tomorrow's activity. Beau says the weather is supposed to clear by this afternoon."

"Oh! Yes, good! It'll bring people back for a second day. Better sales for the vendors." Nancy walked away, congratulating herself on her brilliant idea.

Sam and Linda exchanged a smile, and Sam edged away when three more customers showed up for their free cider samples. She spotted Beau and wandered toward him. The heavenly scent of fresh-roasted green chile grabbed her attention and she followed her nose to Taos Bits and Bites, where Lucy Garcia and a helper were pulling baking pans of hot cheese bread minis from the oven.

"Oh, wow. That looks fabulous," Sam said.

"I'm sure you make just as good at your place, Sam."

"Well, everyone's recipe is a little different. I'd love to try one, as soon as they're cooled enough."

"Five minutes," Lucy said. "You really want to eat these while they're warm." She looked over Sam's shoulder, smiling. "Sheriff, you should have one too."

"How's everything going for you today, Lucy? Any more grumbling among the chefs?"

"I was going to ask you the same thing. Have you figured out what happened to Nando?"

Beau shook his head. "Not really. We don't know who sneaked the poison into the taquitos in his booth. Have you heard anything at all?"

Her eyes became moist, remembering the celebrity chef. "I would let you know if I did. Anyone who would harm such a wonderful man is a horrible, horrible person."

She scooped up two of the little flaky pastries and set each on a napkin. "Here, on the house."

They thanked her and walked on, devouring the small pastries in about two bites. Sam kept her voice low. "So, was that true back there? No new leads today?"

"Darlin' I've only been here for an hour this morning.

So far, Lucy is the only one of the chefs to express sorrow about what happened, though. Rory Jennings plainly thinks Rodriguez was overrated as a chef and was thriving only because of his past television appearances. Aaron Finsted and his wife are no fans either." He wadded up the used paper napkin and tossed it into a nearby bin. "Could be the uniform. No one wants to talk much to me."

"Well, you're hardly grilling them. Maybe that's actually what you should be doing." Her grin belied the serious words. "I'll hang around, see what I can pick up."

A microphone made a shrill squawk as a fingernail tapped it. "Woo, sorry about that," Nancy Whitson said. "I wasn't sure this thing was on."

She stood on the slightly raised dais at the end of the room nearest the kitchen, flashing her smile over the crowd as people looked in that direction.

"I have some announcements, everyone. First of all, we have to apologize for not already having the bouncy pumpkin set up outside. Thanks to Mother Nature's gift of snow this morning, we'll be doing that activity for the kids tomorrow instead. So, moms and dads, we know you'll find lots of great items here among the booths, and that will be your chance to come back for anything you missed today."

She shuffled some index cards from one hand to the other. "Okay, now for the exciting news of the day. As you know our inaugural event is called the Harvest Feast, and there's a wonderful reason for that. Our visiting chefs have been working on some fabulous new recipes, things you can't get in their restaurants."

She turned to her left, waving an arm toward Rory Jennings. "From the Piñon Tree Lodge in Santa Fe—Rory Jennings!"

He took a little bow and waved to the crowd.

"Next along the line is our own Taos Bits and Bites, with Lucy Garcia!" As Nancy continued around the room with the introductions, most of the crowd didn't seem to notice there was an empty space where Casa de Rodriguez had once been set up.

"Now that you've met all of our fabulous chefs, I'll remind you that this year's theme is What To Do With Thanksgiving Leftovers!"

A wave of laughter went through the room.

"Laugh if you will, but I tell you these people have come up with some amazing treats. Throughout the day, each of the chefs will be preparing and handing out samples. And we want you to vote. The chef with the most votes earns the title of Celebrity Chef and gets a cash prize. The competition is fierce, so be sure to sample every dish and turn in your votes on the little ballots available at the Chamber booth. Votes will be tallied and the prizes awarded tomorrow at noon."

Her face was flushed as she thanked the audience and the chefs. "Let the sampling begin!"

As Nancy stepped down from the platform, Sam sensed a commotion near the kitchen door. A heavyset man was pushing his way toward Nancy. Something told Sam this was trouble and she worked her way against the tide of attendees who were heading toward the food booths.

"So this is what was going on while I was away," the man accused, his voice rising dangerously. He waved a sheet of paper toward Nancy.

"Harvey … not here." The words came out through clenched teeth.

"Oh you've already made a spectacle of yourself, *honey*. I'm not the cause of this trouble."

Sam approached from the left and saw Beau coming toward her from the right.

"Problem, sir?" Beau kept his tone casual.

The man flashed the page at them, revealing a professional eight-by-ten photograph of Nando Rodriguez. Sam caught the fact it was autographed but couldn't tell what it said. "Seems my *wife* has a fancy *boyfriend*."

"Can we talk about this in the kitchen?" Sam suggested, spreading her arms to usher them away from the crowded room.

Nancy eagerly headed that way and her husband didn't have much choice but to go along, although Sam sensed he'd have rather remained the center of attention, in order to humiliate Nancy as publicly as possible.

Once the doors swung shut, Beau went into full-on sheriff mode, confronting Harvey Whitson while Sam stood protectively between him and Nancy. "All right, sir, please calm down. And you should be aware that the man in this picture is now dead."

"What?"

"Murdered, this week. I'll need to know where you were on Monday and Tuesday." He gave the man a firm stare.

"Nancy can tell you. I was on a business trip to Dallas. My flight home on Wednesday got delayed."

"We'll check that out. I'll need the name of your hotel and your flight numbers, both coming and going."

Harvey's bluster was gone and he turned toward Nancy for corroboration. She merely looked at him and shrugged.

Beau turned to her. "Can you verify this?"

"It's what he told me. As you know, I was here setting up for the festival." Her eyes beseeched Beau and Sam not to bring up the affair she had confessed to.

Generally, Sam knew, Beau left personal matters for families to sort out unless there was a direct connection to his cases or someone was in danger.

Whitson pulled out his phone and scrolled through emails until he found what he was looking for. "There's my hotel receipt. Last Sunday, Monday, and Tuesday nights. I was supposed to fly home Wednesday but as I said …"

Some more scrolling and he came up with an image of his boarding pass for American Airlines. It wasn't definitive proof he'd actually boarded the flight, but most likely that would check out as well.

"All right, sir. Thank you for providing those. I'd suggest you go on home now."

As Harvey flashed an angry look toward Nancy and stomped out the back door, Sam thought she caught Beau's thoughts reflected in his expression: *there went a viable suspect.*

"Nancy, will you be okay?" Sam asked.

"He signed the photo *with love*," she said with a sigh. "I shouldn't have kept it."

"True. You've got a difficult conversation ahead of you," Beau told her. "If you believe you're in physical danger, let me know. I can have a deputy accompany you home."

Nancy shook her head. "Harvey is mostly all verbal. He shouts and threatens but the abuse is mental rather than physical."

Sam's heart went out to the woman. "Give him time to settle down and then be really clear about what result you want before you talk to him about this."

"I'll think about it. Meanwhile, it's better for me to stay here a while and take my mind off my miserable home life." She turned and pushed through the swinging doors.

"Oh, what tangled webs people weave …" Beau watched her leave.

"What's your gut feeling? Do you think he rigged the poisoned food?"

He shook his head. "I doubt it."

"And do you think he'll get violent with Nancy when they're alone?"

"I'm going to keep an eye on her. When she gets ready to leave for the day, I'll suggest she stay at a hotel until she's ready to decide how the rest of their marriage will go. If she insists on going home, I'll follow along to let him see she has protection."

They walked back into the main room exactly when a scream split the air.

Chapter 11

Sam's attention went to the north wall of the barn, where angry voices were raised.

"You did that on purpose!" It was Chelsea Finsted's voice, and she was staring daggers at Ricky Serna.

He backed away, hands up in a don't-shoot-me position.

Beau and Sam rushed over to see what was happening. A huge crockery pot was smashed on the floor and a stew of some kind had splattered everywhere. People were reaching for paper napkins and wiping the food off their pantlegs and shoes.

"You little rat," Chelsea yelled. "You deliberately knocked that off our countertop."

Mild-mannered Ricky turned to Beau, his eyes pleading. "I didn't. My arm bumped the cookpot, but it was already near the edge. It went over before I could grab it."

"A whole morning's work, shot." This time it was Aaron's voice. "Our green chile turkey stew was getting the most votes, and you deliberately sabotaged us."

"Okay, okay," Beau said. "Everyone settle down. Sam, is there a cleanup crew for such mishaps? Maybe you can find someone to help out?"

She didn't know the answer but she could ask Nancy. As she turned toward the Chamber of Commerce booth, she heard Beau trying to separate the battling chefs. By the time Sam returned with two volunteers with brooms and mops and buckets, he'd cautioned Ricky Serna to stay in his booth while he spoke to the Finsteds outside.

She made her way to the exit, reassuring the other booth holders that it would be fine. Big Range Cookin' was serving up turkey enchiladas in a red chile sauce that smelled fantastic, and Lucy had attracted a good-sized crowd with her deep-fried stuffing canapes at Taos Bits and Bites. One of the artists was carefully examining her paintings for stew splatters, but everyone else seemed to be handling the catastrophe pretty well.

Sam found Beau outside at the corner of the building, listening to Aaron and Chelsea.

"I'm tempted to pack up and go home," Aaron was saying.

Chelsea nudged his side. "But what about—" Her side-eye gaze must have meant something.

Beau caught the motion. "What about what?"

Both of the Finsteds shuffled a little.

"Anything that pertains to this festival might pertain to what happened on Tuesday. If it's nothing to do with Hernando Rodriguez, you'll need to reassure me of that."

No one spoke.

"Okay then, maybe you're right. If you want to leave

the festival, though, it'll be to come down to my office and make this discussion official. None of the visiting chefs are leaving town until we have answers."

Aaron uttered a curse under his breath. He did a little chin-tilt toward his wife.

"Okay," Chelsea said, "if you must know. There's a big investor here, a venture capital firm from California that's looking toward taking a northern New Mexico restaurant and franchising it. It'll be the newest fast-casual sensation. They plan to introduce two dozen restaurants from the west coast and into Arizona and Nevada. If it takes off, they'll go nationwide within five years. They came specifically to the Harvest Feast because Nancy had recruited the best of the best in this part of the state."

"And there's big money in this deal for whichever restaurant is chosen …" The picture was becoming clearer in Sam's head.

"We've put so much into developing new recipes, and winning the popular vote here would be *the* way to let these guys see why they should choose The Savory Duck over any of the others."

"Let me guess. Nando was in the lead in this competition—"

"Because he was the reason they came here in the first place." Chelsea's mouth turned downward. "Face it, he had the national exposure, the reputation."

"Even if he was a jerk," Aaron added. "But being a nice guy isn't worth a damn if someone's looking to fund a successful business."

"Do all the competing chefs know about these investors being here and what's at stake?" Beau watched their faces carefully.

"I don't know about Lucy Garcia. She's everyone's little sweetheart and doesn't seem to have a competitive bone in her body. But for sure, Rory, the Carlsons at Big Range, Ricky, and us—yeah. We're all hoping Nando's loss is our gain." Chelsea swallowed hard. "I didn't mean that how it sounded. We didn't want to see Nando *die*. We all kind of wished he'd go away so the rest of us would have a fair chance."

"Enough to slip in a little poison to make him sick?" Beau's voice had an edge to it now.

"No! No no *no*. I mean, *we* didn't." She waved her hand back and forth between herself and her husband. "I have no idea how far anyone else would go."

"Did you see or hear anything specific, someone threatening him or messing around in his booth as he was getting set up for the show?"

Both of them shook their heads. "Our booth is clear across the way from his. We were scrambling to get our own setup done."

Beau let out a long breath. "Okay. You decide if you want to go back in there, put on a smile, and keep competing. But don't leave town yet."

Aaron muttered about how they might as well go back and figure out another dish to make. Sam watched the couple go back into the barn.

"Well, it's a new wrinkle, but hardly a surprise where Nando was concerned. With the debt he'd accumulated, it had to be super important for him to win over these investors."

"I'm phoning in a request for background checks on all the other vendors. Anyone else with big financial problems would have an excellent motive." He got Rico on the line and explained, giving authorization for credit checks on both business and personal accounts.

"I'm heading back inside to taste the creations and decide who I'll vote for," Sam said with a wink in his direction.

The first familiar faces she saw when she walked in were Kelly, Scott, and Anastasia, her granddaughter. "We decided we had to come check it out. Maybe we'll find some new recipes to include in our own Thanksgiving dinner."

That led to a discussion of who was bringing what for their dinner on Sunday afternoon, and of course Sam had to ask how Scott's latest book was coming along. His children's mystery series featuring Maddie Plimpton, girl detective, had become hugely popular ever since he left his college professorship to become an author.

As Scott and Ana moved away to check out the booths, Kelly asked how the investigation was going.

"A dozen suspects and a couple of strong motives. No answers."

"Is Beau regretting his decision to accept his old job back?"

"Not for a moment. At least I don't think he is." Sam scanned the room and saw he'd come back inside and was lingering near the Farmer's Table booth where Ricky Serna was keeping his distance from his neighbors, the Finsteds.

Even at this distance she could see that they'd fashioned a sign "Stew Tomorrow!" while they'd apparently come up with something else to prepare and serve, putting the best face on the earlier mess. It must have worked. Two men who, even in casual clothing, were easily pegged as the visiting Californians, were standing at the booth and chatting with a smiling Chelsea.

By the time the venue closed at four p.m., Sam was dead on her feet and not at all hungry, the upside of patrolling a food fair with lots of tasty treats to sample. She and Beau were on the way out to their vehicles when his phone rang.

"It's Lisa. Looks like I may be a few minutes behind you." He saw Sam out to her vehicle while he took the call.

The department's forensic technician and crime scene investigator must have had more than just a quick report, Sam decided, when Beau didn't get home right away. He called to say Lisa had been on her way to the Lone Tree and he'd waited for her. More evidence needed to be collected.

Sam used the extra hour to shower and change into soft sweats before helping herself to a glass of wine. If her husband was agreeable, a TV movie and a bowl of popcorn would solve the questions of both dinner and entertainment.

As it turned out, she was dozing on the sofa at nine o'clock when Beau finally walked in.

"Whew—a lot more work than I anticipated." He pulled off his sheepskin jacket and hung it on the rack by the door. "The original fingerprint results were inconclusive and Lisa suggested taking more prints and trying to gather some DNA for testing. Since all the participants are only in town one more day we decided to get on the task right away."

Sam stood and stretched, to wake herself up and get her head back into the subject of the murder case. "Are you hungry? We can come up with something."

He declined. "The interesting thing is that there were a few other prints in the Rodriguez booth, other than Nando's and Josie's. Lisa had already taken those, but we had nothing to match them to. So we went around to all the other vendors and found items they would have touched, but their customers wouldn't have—cooking pots, knives, that sort of thing. We dusted absolutely everything and labeled it all."

"So if any of the other vendors went into Nando's booth, messing around with stuff, you'll know who it is."

"Exactly."

"You're feeling pretty sure it's one of them?"

"Has to be someone associated with the festival, someone with access to his booth and the supplies he brought in. He died on the day they were all there setting up." He yawned and pulled Sam close. "It's a huge task, and I'm thankful not to be the person back in the lab who has to go through all the evidence right now."

"You're exhausted. Let's head upstairs."

* * *

It was well after eight in the morning when they woke up. Beau put on jeans and a work shirt and headed toward the corral to look after the horses and give Danny Flores his instructions for the day. Sam called the bakery to check in. The wedding cake delivery was the big item on the agenda. She told Becky she would come by, load it in the van, and get it to the reception venue on time.

"Don't worry about it, Sam. We managed several of these while you were out of town, and I'm sure we can handle this one. Julio will help me get it loaded in the van and someone at the other end can assist if I need them."

"Call me, though, if you need me." Sam looked out the window to see Beau heading back toward the house. "I know Beau wants extra eyes on the people in this festival, but he can surely spare me for a while."

"I will call. But don't worry."

Once again, Beau dressed in his uniform, and they took two vehicles. Sam wasn't looking forward to another long day of strolling among the same booths, looking at the same crafts, but she reminded herself it would be a great chance to get some advance Christmas shopping done. Plus, all of the chefs in the competition had promised new dishes today, and it could be interesting and fun to see what they came up with.

When the doors opened at ten, a good-sized crowd had already gathered. Kids were going at it with the bouncy-castle shaped like a pumpkin in the parking lot, as Nancy Whitson had promised. The Chamber director stood nearby, looking a bit more haggard than yesterday at this time. Sam walked over to say hello and check on her.

"I stayed at a hotel last night. Harvey called, not quite remorseful for throwing such a fit yesterday. I apologized a hundred times for what I'd done. In retrospect, getting involved with Nando was a stupid mistake."

"Maybe you and Harvey can work things out."

"I don't know. He's a man who holds onto anger.. *Grudge* should have been his middle name."

Again, Sam wondered how far such a grudge might go. She made a mental note to mention this to Beau so he could keep an eye on Harvey Whitson. They had no idea how long ago he'd discovered the signed photograph so, in her opinion, he was still high on the suspect list.

Inside the barn, delicious smells filled the air once again. She walked over to the Taos Bits and Bites booth to say hello to Lucy.

"I've come up with a chile glaze for turkey legs," the

young chef told her. "Try a taste?"

She cut the meat off some of the glazed legs, as samples, and Sam moaned with pleasure as the sweet-hot flavors hit her tongue. "Oh wow. Yum!"

"It's also a great way to glaze the entire turkey while roasting it," Lucy suggested. "I'm selling containers of the glaze here, and I'm looking into bottling it and selling it through grocery stores eventually."

"It'll be a hit. I'll take two pints of it now. We're doing a turkey tomorrow for our family dinner, and I'll get these over to Kelly."

Lucy bagged the two pint-sized containers and included a printed slip with other recipe ideas for the glaze. Sam's interest had attracted several more customers and the booth quickly became busy.

Sam moved on to Linda Fresquez's Warm & Fuzzy booth, where she picked up cute hand-knitted mittens for Ana and Kelly. Linda seemed a little distracted this morning.

"Everything okay?"

"Oh yeah, I'm doing great. Sold a lot yesterday. Sorry, I got preoccupied with some of the other vendors. The chefs came in this morning to find black smudges on their gear and were griping about having to clean it up."

"Ah. Right. Beau and the forensics tech had to gather more evidence for their case. I guess they didn't get the chance to brief everyone that it was happening."

"They haven't caught the killer yet, I guess."

"It's not always easy. I know he's worried about everyone getting away before he can ask all the questions he needs to."

"One of the other chefs from Albuquerque was talking

about the funeral, saying it's coming up next week?"

"That's what we heard. I wonder if the other chefs will attend."

Linda's brows furrowed. "I don't know. I don't get the feeling these guys are friends, really."

"Professional jealousy?"

"Yes, I think that's it. They're not like artists and writers, from what I can tell. Those groups tend to be friends, even when they are sort of in direct competition for customers."

Sam had noticed that, too, when she'd met visiting authors in Ivan's bookshop.

"Anyway, I wish you luck in the search." Linda turned toward another woman who was examining a cashmere shawl.

Passing among the booths, Sam picked up gifts—a scented candle for Zoë, an engraved pen set for Scott, a manly knitted watch cap for Julio, and herbal bath salts for the bakery girls. She had gift bags in both hands, proud of herself for getting a jump on the holiday shopping and supporting local artisans at the same time.

As she crossed the large room, a scent caught her attention. Waffles. She drifted toward the Big Range Cookin' booth and said hello to the Carlsons. Three waffle irons were in use, and as each golden square came out, the chefs set it on a plate and dipped a red syrup from a nearby crock.

Cranberry Sauced Waffles was printed on a small placard, and the concoction appeared—by the lineup of people waiting—to be the hit of the show.

"The perfect breakfast for Thanksgiving weekend," Daisy Carlson was telling those in line. "Have a sample or purchase a plateful. And vote for us!"

Sam's slice of toast from home wasn't holding her over, and she decided a waffle would be just the thing. But first, she needed to stash her gift purchases in her truck. She edged past the eager shoppers and spotted Beau near the main entrance.

"Looks like you bought out half the vendors." He looked at the bags in her hands.

"Almost. No peeking. It's all top-secret stuff." She shifted two bags so she could reach into her coat pocket for her keys. "How's it going?"

He shook his head. "Plenty of complaints about the fingerprint dust on their equipment. But it hasn't prompted anyone to turn themselves in. I'm about to give up on this place. Everyone's busy, and none of them are acting suspiciously toward me. And I can accomplish more back at the office."

"No surprise confession by the killer?"

"It never seems to work that way."

"Well, I'm not leaving until I have one of those waffles," she said with a laugh, passing him and heading toward the door. "I'll buy you one if you want to hang around."

The parking lot was even more crowded when she walked out to her truck. Stashing her purchases in the hidden compartment under the back seat, she relocked the vehicle and started back. With visions of those fluffy waffles occupying her mind, she almost bumped into a woman who was pulling a wheeled cart.

"Sorry." She realized the woman was Josie Rodriguez, and she had someone else with her.

Josie seemed to have aged in the past four days. Her hair was lank, with a stripe of gray roots showing, and her eyes looked puffy. Sam's heart went out to her. Grief was such a difficult thing.

The younger woman with Josie was wearing a Casa de Rodriguez logo shirt. Sam guessed she was an employee of the restaurant.

"Josie, how are you doing?"

A blank look, then recognition dawned. "You're …"

"Samantha Sweet. I was here with the sheriff the day it happened. We're so sorry about your loss."

Josie took a firmer grip on the handle of the cart. "I came to get our stuff. That lady said it needed to be cleared out today."

"Yes, true. But we could have gathered your things and stored them for a few days. I know it's a tough time. Beau said the funeral is Wednesday?"

"Right. Well, I'm here now. Carlie will help me, and we have Nando's truck to haul everything home." She turned away.

"Let me know if you need a hand," Sam called out. But the other woman didn't respond.

Okay then. Sam stood inside the barn, watching Josie head directly for the booth. The line for waffles was longer than before—word must have gotten out. She spotted Beau near the Savory Duck booth and tilted her head toward the one across the way, where Josie had now parked her cart.

"What the hell is all this!" It didn't take but a moment for all heads to turn at Josie's exclamation.

Sam hurried over.

"All my equipment is filthy with this black stuff!"

"Um, yes. Sorry about that, but the forensic team had to do some additional dusting."

"And my good stock pot is gone. What the hell?" Josie stomped around the little kitchenette, rattling pans and kicking over a stool. Her assistant scooted to the side, wide-eyed.

"Let's check with Beau. Here he comes." Sam felt a little unnerved by the woman's anger, although she supposed that was also one of the ways in which grief came out.

Beau walked over, straightening his shoulders as he quietly told the onlookers to go back to whatever they were doing. He approached the booth and gave Josie a steady gaze. "Sorry for the mess—it couldn't be helped."

"This is ridiculous! What did you do with all the food we brought?"

"Ma'am, it's a murder investigation. All the food items had to be tested for contamination, then destroyed." He kept his voice low and firm. "There are certain procedures we have to follow. We all feel sympathy for your family, but it's in everyone's best interest to find the facts and get the case solved as quickly as possible."

His phone chimed with an incoming text message. He gave it a quick glance, tensing, and thumbed one of the numbers in his recent call list.

"Lisa … little busy right now …" He listened for three seconds. "A dark red pan? What—"

Sam's ears tuned to him but her eyes stayed on the women in the booth.

Josie made a dismissive sound and turned her back, reaching toward something on the back counter, and Sam spotted an expensive Le Creuset skillet in red enamel. But instead of the pan, Josie came back with a large knife from the block on the counter.

Chapter 12

Beau jammed his phone into Sam's hands, took a step back, and placed a hand on his holstered weapon. "Put the knife down, ma'am. Right now."

Josie's assistant took a giant step backward and Beau's attention momentarily switched to her. Sam's heart thudded. The call with Lisa was still active. "Send immediate backup to the Lone Tree Barn. Suspect is armed," she instructed, sticking the phone into her pocket.

"I've got this one. You watch Josie," she murmured to Beau, stepping over to the wide-eyed girl who didn't seem to have a clue what was going on.

Without taking his eyes off the knife, Beau flicked the safety snap on his holster and closed his hand around the grip on his pistol.

"Josie … don't do anything rash." His voice was frosty.

"Put the knife down."

Her hand began to waver and her lower lip trembled. "I didn't mean it. I didn't want—"

"Knife down, then we'll talk."

But Josie gritted her teeth and took another step forward. Beau stepped back and pulled his weapon. Sam shoved the assistant aside and grabbed a smaller skillet by its handle. In one quick move, she swung the skillet down on Josie's wrist. The knife clattered to the floor.

Beau kicked it out of the way, holstering his pistol and reaching for the handcuffs on his belt, all in one motion.

"Josie Rodriguez, you're under arrest for threatening an officer of the law."

"That's it?" Sam's eyes were wide.

"Oh, she'll be booked on suspicion of murder too, don't worry. We'll get the whole story down at the station."

By the time Rico and Lawson arrived, the handcuffed Josie was standing beside Beau's cruiser and her assistant was sitting inside, weeping. Beau escorted their suspect to Rico's vehicle. Josie kept muttering incomprehensible things about her brother. The three law enforcement vehicles left the property, forming a little convoy toward town.

Sam stepped back into the festival venue, carrying the roll of crime scene tape Beau had left with her. As she advanced upon the Rodriguez booth, Nancy Whitson approached. Her lipstick stood out in sharp contrast to the pallor of her face. A cluster of people stood around, gawking.

"Nancy, maybe you can say something to get everyone's mind back on the festival? Encourage them to try the food, announce the winners of the contest … whatever it is you need to keep your event on track."

"But—"

"The sheriff believes he's got the killer, but … this doesn't need to become news around town right now. We need to let justice take its course. So, talk about any subject except this one, okay?"

For once, Nancy didn't protest and she followed instructions. By the time Sam wrapped the yellow tape around the booth, Nancy's voice over the microphone had pulled the crowd to that end of the space. Sam slipped quietly out the door.

Chapter 13

The kitchen in Kelly's large Victorian home bustled with activity and brimmed over with the scents of the holiday, and despite the fact that Sam had just spent several days surrounded by these foods, there was something special about the fact that this was family and home. Savoring the frosty quiet of a Sunday, she and Beau arrived a touch before noon to help Kelly with preparations for the meal that was planned for two p.m.

They'd parked Sam's truck under the portico and walked in through the kitchen door to find Kelly, Riki, and Sam's best friend Zoë busy around the stove.

"Turkey comes out in an hour," Kelly announced, "so you might as well relax with the guys in the living room."

Five-year-old Ana dashed in and grabbed Sam around the waist. "Grammy, we're having Coke Jello!"

"Definitely a once-a-year treat," Kelly inserted. "There's so much sugar in it, no one can handle it more often."

Sam laughed and hugged her granddaughter. "And what else?"

"Eliza might be having kittens."

Okay, that was a complete about-turn in subjects.

"Eliza is not having any babies, honey. I know you wish she would, but she can't. Remember that vet appointment? Oh, you probably don't. We got Eliza before we had you." Kelly brushed a wayward curl from her forehead and turned back to the large saucepan of gravy on the stove. "Maybe you can take Grandpa Beau in and show him where your daddy and Uncle Darryl are."

In another shift of energy, Ana grabbed Beau's hand and tugged him toward the dining room door. In the distance, Sam heard the front doorbell ring.

"That's gotta be either Emily or Rupert. They're the only others we invited this year."

"I'm so glad you decided on Sunday for the big dinner." Zoë scooted Kelly aside to peek into the oven at the progress of the sweet potatoes. "Thursday is always an awkward day for us, since the B&B usually has guests and we have our tradition of feeding them more than breakfast that day."

"We're glad you could come." Kelly turned to Sam. "So, I understand you and Beau solved your case?"

"We did." She related the dramatic episode where Josie had pulled the knife on Beau and he'd stayed calm, making light of her own role in whacking the woman's wrist to make her drop the weapon. "As far as what happened next, I'll have to defer to Beau. Maybe later, over dinner. He still hasn't told me exactly what happened once they took her to the station."

And that's how it went. Dinner was served, plates heaped high, exclamations made over the wonderful dishes. Once Ana took off to find a holiday movie on Nickelodeon and the adults settled in with pie and coffee, Kelly pressed for the details. "How on earth did you figure out it was the sister?"

Sam wasn't at all sure how to answer that—aside from the facts that the toxic substance had only been found in their booth and the chef had been extremely picky about letting anyone else near his cooking station, the other clues were so much more subtle. She sent a smile toward Beau. "Please—I'm curious what she told you once you had her in custody. Out there at the Lone Tree, she kept saying she didn't mean it."

"Right. She stuck with that for a while, but when Lisa explained exactly how deadly that substance was, she cracked. Said she only meant to make her brother sick so he'd have to bow out of the competition. She had spiked the turkey taquito filling mixture and personally rolled one of the little appetizers to be sure it was the one he would eat. She claimed she had this idea that when he tasted it, he would become too ill to stay. She would discard the bad filling and proceed through the festival without him in the way. She wanted the limelight for herself, to make people see that Casa de Rodriguez's success was equally due to her hard work."

Sam nodded. "I got that impression, that Nando was a glory-hog, never gracious about sharing credit with anyone else."

"Josie knew the potential investors from California were there, and that was another thing. She said she was really scared they would choose Nando as their celebrity representative, give him a lot of money to license the restaurant for franchises, and then he'd gamble it all away. She's no dummy. She has a pretty good idea how much he was into the loan sharks for, and that his addiction would continue to burn through all the cash he could get hold of."

"But to kill him? Couldn't she have just let them know, quietly maybe, that they'd be risking the restaurant's success if they gave her brother a huge sum of cash?"

"There's more, and this has nothing to do with any investors or debt."

"What?" Kelly's eyes widened.

"In the Rodriguez family, it's tradition that the eldest son inherits everything. An archaic idea, dating back to a time when women routinely died in childbirth and the man of the house took over. If a woman was widowed, his brothers would see to it she was taken care of …"

"Sounds very sixteen-hundreds to me," Zoë said.

"Well, no matter. Apparently, Josie found out their mother had adhered to this way of thinking and her will completely cut Josie out. She and Hernando were the only children, and the only way for Josie to inherit anything at all was if her brother predeceased her."

Sam's fingers rose to her lips. "Oh my gosh. The mother is quite elderly now and not in good health, right? I think that's what we were told. So, Josie was reaching the now-or-never point. Nando had been married several times and most likely had some kids scattered about. Once he inherited, there would be a line of succession, and Josie would be dependent upon the generosity of people she barely knew."

"And the fate of the restaurant would probably be

sealed. Too much debt, no celebrity backing for the investors, and no way Josie could finance its survival on her own." Beau set his coffee cup down.

"And now?" Kelly's voice dropped. "This is all so sad. Josie will still lose everything."

"Knowing the motive about the inheritance and the will, I doubt there's a lawyer in the country who could spin this premeditated act of hers into anything less than first-degree murder," Beau said.

Kelly's husband, Scott, always the quiet one at the table, piped up. "There could be one bright spot. I'm no lawyer, but I used to teach a section on heirs and succession in my history classes. Granted, that had mostly to do with the royal side of things, mainly from our state's connection with Spain. But depending on how the old woman's will is written, her money would probably still go to Josie. Although she'll be behind bars forever, the money could be used to pay off the family debts and to keep the restaurant going. Which could hold some appeal for the investors as far as a potential franchising deal."

"I don't know … sounds complicated," Zoë added.

"It is, and I have no idea how it will go." Beau looked around the table. "Nando Rodriguez was not known for sharing his recipes, and Josie is probably the only one familiar with his cooking techniques. Most likely, this will be an irrevocable stain on Casa de Rodriguez, and the shiny reputation of Nando will be lost to time."

Emily and Rupert had been quietly clearing the table and dividing the leftover food into take-home packets, and when all were back at the dining table, Darryl was the one who spoke first.

"Ladies, that was a fabulous dinner and we thank you

all. Now, as for me, I think a walk is in order. Who's coming with?"

Scott alone opted to stretch out on the couch with Ana for the ending of her movie, while the others slipped their jackets on and headed down the long driveway toward the dirt road. Sam found herself walking between Beau and Riki, while Kelly, Emily, Darryl, and Zoë chatted ahead of them.

"How are you doing, Riki?" Sam lightly touched the younger woman's shoulder. "It was different not having Evan here."

"It was. But I shall be all right. It's a quieter life, that's for sure." Riki turned toward Beau. "And what about you? I imagine you didn't plan on dealing with a murder case immediately after the mayor's swearing-in ceremony."

Beau thought about it for a long moment. "One thing about this job, you never know what will come up. The weekend could have just as easily meant nothing more than handing out a dozen traffic tickets. But to answer your question—it feels good to be back."

Sam smiled. She had noticed how much Beau brightened when he was following the career he'd dedicated so much of his life to. In uniform, his shoulders were straighter, his step more resilient, his voice firmer. There would be an election next year, when the people would decide whether he kept the job, but for now it was his.

She reached for his hand with both of hers. "You are exactly where you want to be and I love you, Sheriff Cardwell."

Author's Note

First and foremost, I want to thank my editor, Stephanie Dewey, and her fabulous team of beta readers who always come through with insightful comments and great catches for the boo-boos in my manuscripts. To Isobel Tamney, Marcia Koopmann, Sandra Anderson, Paula Webb, and Susan Gross—thank you so much! You're the best!

This story was a fun one, coming up with foods and a slightly different spin on Thanksgiving. I must warn you, many of the dishes I mentioned in the narrative of the story are fictional, as far as I know. If one of those names sparked your imagination and you decide to invent it, please let me know and send me a copy of your recipe!

And now, for some real recipes. I reached out to my mailing list with a request for submissions, and a number of fans came back with their favorites. My editorial team went through and chose the best of the best, and I've included them in the following pages, along with a few that are favorites in my family, as well.

Thankful Sweets – Recipes from readers

Marcia gets top honors for really and truly using up the Thanksgiving leftovers with this one!

Thanksgiving Shepherd's Pie - from Marcia K.

Our favorite way to use up the leftovers is really flexible. It's a variation on Shepherd's Pie. Start with a baking dish that will hold several layers.

I use the leftover dressing/stuffing as the crust or base.
Next I add the turkey, use however much you want but enough for a decent layer.
Top that with a layer of vegetables, whatever you have left. If I serve brussels sprouts or broccoli as the vegetable, I put frozen corn, peas or green beans in instead.
Next up is the gravy. Pour it over the top of the veggies. Use enough to soak the lower layers.
I usually mash sweet potatoes as well as white potatoes, so put those on top of the gravy in stripes or sections and top it with pats of butter.

Bake at 350 for about 40 minutes until heated through.

Can be made ahead and refrigerated. If you do this, it may take a bit longer to heat completely.

Variations I have done in the past include sprinkling the top with various cheeses (especially if the sweet potatoes are gone. I have also added a mix of green chiles and jalapeno peppers chopped up and mixed in with the turkey layer to give it a bit of a kick. Use whatever chile peppers you prefer. When I do the chiles, I lightly sprinkle some cumin into the mashed potatoes (both white and sweet) before I layer them on.

Serve with cranberry relish or sauce on the side, along with a green salad.

**Connie's note: Marcia tells me this one is so popular with her family that they encourage her to make it at other times of the year, using packaged stuffing mix and turkey or chicken from the deli!

~ ~ ~ ~

Grilled Turkey & Cheese sandwiches – from Elaine P.

It's pretty simple:
Butter 2 slices of bread & lay one, butter side down, in a heated skillet. Place a slice of your favorite cheese (we like a white cheese like provolone or Swiss), then layer as much turkey as you can handle on the cheese! My husband loves to put leftover bread dressing on his.

To "Southwest it up," put some roasted, peeled Hatch chile on top of the turkey. Top with the other slice of bread, and grill bread to your liking.

~ ~ ~ ~

Spicy Turkey Pot Pie – from Chenier

1lb cut up leftover turkey
4 small diced cooked potatoes
1/2 can green peas
1/2 cup diced carrots
1 can cream of chicken soup
1 diced jalapeno (as much or little as you like)
Garlic & onion powder to taste
Salt & pepper optional

Mix in a pot, heat & serve with cranberry sauce, hot biscuits & butter
(You can also use chicken, ham or meatless)

Fresh Cranberry Relish – from Cynthia B.

2 bags fresh cranberries
4 oranges
1-1/2 cups sugar

Grind cranberries in a food processor. Medium grind.
Place in a large bowl.
Slice oranges into eight pieces. Grind them medium grind in a food processor rind and all.
Mix cranberries, oranges and sugar in a bowl.

Let sit covered in the refrigerator for 2 days in order to let the flavors blend.
This freezes very well.

~ ~ ~ ~

~ ~ ~ ~

Mexican Corn Pudding – from Elyse W.

1 can corn (drained, 15oz)
1 can cream style corn, 15oz
1 can Hatch green chiles
Salt and pepper to taste
½ lb. cheese (grated)
1½ cups milk
3 tablespoons corn starch
4 beaten eggs
3 tablespoons butter, melted
Bread crumbs

Combine all ingredients; pour in a greased baking dish and sprinkle bread crumbs over the top. Cook in a moderately hot oven until firm to the touch and knife comes out clean. 375' for 45+ minutes

~ ~ ~ ~

Sweet Potato Southwest from Mike H.

Two sweet potatoes cooked and mashed (with peeling, cut up, or without) or use canned sweet potatoes
One to one and a half cups whole kernel corn (cooked frozen is my favorite)
Mix those together well.
Add vegan margarine (or your favorite)
Add maple syrup to taste
Add salsa (your choice of heat) to taste

Mix well. Heat for a short time together.
Enjoy this healthy and delicious favorite of mine.

* Added note: Mike's favorite way to cook the potatoes: Slice the raw sweet potatoes into disks about ¾ to 1 inch thick (after cutting off a half inch or so on each end.) Place the slices into a covered microwave dish with ¼ to ½ inch of water. Steam in a microwave for about 14 minutes (900 W) Container and contents will be hot. Drain water. Cut off peeling or cut each circle of peeling into several pieces. Mash the potatoes. Continue with adding cooked corn, margarine, maple syrup, and salsa. I have shared this at church potlucks to good reviews.

Chicken Tortilla Casserole – from Jan S.

Serves 6

4-5 large cooked, chopped chicken breasts
*1 can cream of mushroom soup
*1 can cream of chicken soup
2 - 3 ounce cans chopped green chiles, drained
1 cup black olives, sliced (optional)
1/2 teaspoon garlic salt
1 small onion, chopped very fine (optional)
*1 cup sour cream
1/2 teaspoon garlic salt
salt and pepper to taste
3/4 pkg (8 oz) Taco flavored chips, crushed
*12 ounces shredded sharp cheese

Mix all ingredients except cheese; place in 3 quart casserole -sprinkle cheese on top and bake 30 minutes at 350 degrees.
Can be prepared and frozen unbaked.
Serve with taco toppings (lettuce, tomato, sour cream, cheese, taco sauce, or whatever toppings you like).

* You can use low fat soup, sour cream and cheese. Also, I divide the shredded cheese and mix part in the chicken mixture and put the rest on the top for baking.

~ ~ ~ ~

Mom's Super Brownies – from Gina N.

1-1/2 cups granulated sugar
3/4 cup all-purpose flour
2/3 cup cocoa powder
1/2 cup powered sugar
1/2 cup dark chocolate chips
3/4 teaspoon sea salt
2 large eggs
1/2 cup canola oil or extra-virgin olive oil
2 tablespoons water
1/2 teaspoon Mexican vanilla
1 tablespoon of ancho chile powder

Instructions:

1. Preheat the oven to 325°F. Lightly spray an 8x8 baking dish (not a 9x9 dish or your brownies will overcook) with cooking spray and line it with parchment paper. Spray the parchment paper.
2. In a medium bowl, combine the sugar, flour, cocoa powder, powdered sugar, chocolate chips, and salt.
3. In a large bowl, whisk together the eggs, olive oil, water, and vanilla.
4. Sprinkle the dry mix over the wet mix and stir until just combined.
5. Pour the batter into the prepared pan (it'll be thick - that's ok) and use a spatula to smooth the top. Bake for 40 to 48 minutes, or until a toothpick comes out with only a few crumbs attached. Don't overcook them, otherwise they will be hard and dry. Cool completely before slicing.

You can add 1/2 cup of Dulce de Leche on top of the brownie mix in the pan and use a knife to swirl it into the brownie mix. If you do this decrease the granulated sugar to 1 cup.. Unless you like things super sweet.

And now, some favorites of the Shelton household!

Fabulously Easy Sticky Buns

(perfect for Thanksgiving morning!)

½ c. butter or margarine
½ c. chopped nuts
1 c. brown sugar, packed
2 T. water
2 cans refrigerated crescent dinner rolls

Preheat oven to 375. Using a 12-cup tube pan or bundt pan (not one with a removable bottom), sprinkle 3 tablespoons of the nuts in the bottom. In a saucepan, melt the butter. Add remaining nuts, brown sugar and water to the butter; heat to boiling, stirring occasionally.

Remove crescent rolls from cans—do not unroll the dough. Cut each section into four slices (16 slices total). Arranges 8 slices in the tube pan, separating each pinwheel slightly to allow sauce to penetrate. Spoon half the caramel sauce over the dough. Top with remaining dough slices and remaining sauce. Bake 25-30 minutes until deep golden brown. Cool three minutes. Turn upside down onto a serving platter. Enjoy!

~ ~ ~ ~

Cherry Coke Jello

(At every holiday, it's my hubby's personal favorite!)

1 pkg Black Cherry Jello
1 can pitted dark sweet cherries
8 oz Coca Cola
½ c. chopped pecans

Drain the syrup from the cherries into a large microwave-safe measuring cup. Add water, if needed, to make 1 cup of liquid. Heat to near-boiling. Place the black cherry Jello into a serving bowl and add the hot liquid, stirring until gelatin is dissolved. Add the 8 oz of Coke and stir (it will foam up!). Add the cherries—whole or chopped, your choice. Stir in the chopped pecans. Chill until gelatin is set.

~ ~ ~ ~

Serena's Sweet Potatoes and Apples

4 sweet potatoes – sliced, peel them or not—your choice
3 apples sliced – peeled or not
1/4 cup sugar (we like Mexican sugar which is less refined, similar to Sugar in the Raw)
1/3 cup butter
1/2 tsp cinnamon

Place sliced sweet potatoes and apples in a baking dish. Sprinkle with sugar, dot with butter, sprinkle with cinnamon. Bake in 350 degree oven for about an hour or until potatoes and apples are tender.

Maple Sweet Potatoes

1 can sweet potatoes, drained
2 T. butter
2 T. pure maple syrup
½ t. pumpkin pie spice
salt and pepper
chopped toasted pecans
additional maple syrup

Place drained sweet potatoes in a microwave safe bowl. Cover and heat in micro on high for 5 minutes. Drain and discard any liquid from bowl. Add butter, maple syrup and pumpkin pie spice. Use a fork and mash to combine. Season to taste with salt and pepper. Sprinkle with chopped toasted pecans and drizzle with additional maple syrup.

Start to finish, 10 minutes.
Makes 4 servings and I usually double it (at least) for holidays.

~ ~ ~ ~

Homemade Turkey Soup

This is another simple one. After carving the turkey and storing the meat in zipper bags or freezer containers, I always cook the turkey bones down to make soup. Simply add 1-2 inches of water to the roasting pan and bring it to a boil on the stovetop. Cover and simmer for about 20 minutes.

When the pan has cooled enough to be safe, use two forks to pick the meat from the bones. Toss the skin and bones away and save the broth to use as the base for the best-ever soup. This can be frozen and used at a later date, if desired.

When ready to make the soup, just add veggies of your choosing—canned or frozen mixed vegetables work great—along with chopped onion and garlic, if you like. I also add 4-6 cups of chicken bouillon (depending on how much soup you want to end up with). Season to taste with salt and pepper and simmer for an hour or so. About 15 min before serving, toss in whatever noodles or pasta you like and simmer until the noodles are tender.

**Give it a Southwestern kick by adding either red or green chile when you add the veggies. Instead of pasta, add crispy tortilla strips or chips right before serving.

Serve with garlic bread or warm tortillas. Enjoy!

~ ~ ~ ~

Taco Soup

Easy and Hearty on a cold winter's night!

1-1/2 lbs. lean ground beef (this could work equally well with diced chicken or turkey)
1 large onion, chopped
1 pkg fajita or taco seasoning mix—dry
1 small pkg ranch-style dressing mix—dry
1 can pinto beans
1 can black beans
2 cans diced tomatoes
1 can chopped Hatch green chile – mild or hot, your choice
1 can whole corn
1-1/2 c. water

In a skillet, brown the meat and onion, drain off fat, add dry seasoning mixes. Stir until well mixed. In a stew pot or slow cooker, dump all the canned ingredients, undrained, followed by the meat/onion mixture and water. Stir until well blended. Simmer for about an hour on the stove, or if using slow cooker about 2 hours on High or 4 hours on Low.
Serve with cornbread, garlic bread, or tortillas. Enjoy!

~ ~ ~ ~

Find more of my favorite New Mexico recipes—including Pedro's Green Chile Chicken Enchiladas and Samantha Sweet's Bizcochitos—on my website at connieshelton.com/recipes-from-nm

Thank you for taking the time to read *Thankful Sweets*. If you enjoyed it, please consider telling your friends or posting a short review. Word of mouth is an author's best friend and is much appreciated.

Thank you,

Connie Shelton

~ ~ ~

Sign up for Connie Shelton's free mystery newsletter at connieshelton.com and receive advance information about new books, along with a chance at prizes, discounts and other mystery news!

Contact by email: connie@connieshelton.com

Follow Connie Shelton on Twitter, Pinterest and Facebook

Made in United States
Orlando, FL
04 November 2024